D1559946

Merton Glade

Days of Wine and Murder

DEDALUS

Published by Dedalus in 1984
9 St. Stephen's Terrace, London SW8 1DJ

ISBN 0 946626 06 5

First published by Dedalus in April 1984
First reprint May 1984

Made and printed in Great Britain by
The City Printing Works (Chester-le-Street) Ltd.,
Chester-le-Street, Co. Durham DH3 3NJ.

British Library Cataloguing in Publication Data

Glade, Merton
Days of wine and murder.
I. Title
823'.914(F) PR6057.L2/

ISBN 0-946626-06-5

The characters in this book are ficticious and any resemblance
to anyone either living or dead is purely coincidental.

To Mavis

and for Susan, Steven and Alison

Also by Merton Glade

The ABC of Real Power

They are not long, the days of wine and roses;
Out of a misty dream
Our path emerges for a while, then closes
Within a dream
                    Ernest Dowson

CHAPTER 1

The hardest part would be keeping awake. He would feign sleep to discourage conversation, but at all costs he must stay awake.

As he fastened his seat belt he thought how easy it had been so far. The passport control had been no more than a formality, but nevertheless it had given him confidence.

He took a handful of tissues from the box on his lap and holding them to his face he coughed and spluttered convincingly. The Pakistani passenger next to him edged away.

He looked out of the window as the aircraft started to move and he knew that there could be no turning back. His tongue probed one of the pads in his mouth and his hand strayed to his head touching the lifeless hair. If the wig moved or a mouth pad became dislodged? He must stay awake.

The beautiful Thai hostess was handing out orchids to the women passengers. The Pakistani's wife accepted one with a smile.

"It is a happy idea, I am thinking," the Pakistani said to him.

He grunted in reply and spluttered into his tissues. The Pakistani turned to his wife and spoke rapidly. She looked across her husband and examined the man with the tissues. He was slumped in his seat. Thick black hair falling almost to his wide hornrimmed spectacles, his face all but obscured by the handful of tissues he was holding. She shrugged and neither of them spoke to him again.

* * *

"Good morning, Ladies and Gentlemen. Thai International welcome you aboard this Orchid Service flight London to Bangkok. There will be short stops at Rome and Karachi and we hope you will have a pleasant flight. The safety instructions are . . ." He stopped listening, looked at his watch and mentally checked his timetable for the hundreth time. Leave London Sunday at 7.30 a.m. — he looked again at his watch 7.35 — a good start. Bangkok by 11 o'clock tonight London time, change planes and in Hong Kong by 3.45 a.m. tomorrow morning London time. But as Hong Kong was seven hours ahead of London that made it 10.45 Monday morning. If all went well and the planes were on time, he would leave Hong Kong at 5.45 that same afternoon and be back in London by 7.30 Tuesday morning. Forty-eight hours exactly and allowing for customs, and check-in it would give him over four hours in Hong Kong.

But if there were delays? Then he would have to risk a direct flight by British Airways. That could make up a few hours, but it was more risky. But the whole thing was preposterously risky. No. He must not think of it. Concentrate on the details. On the mechanics. Four hours.

* * *

He shuffled forward in the queue, and glanced at his watch, 4.15. He looked at the large airport clock 11.15. On schedule. His head was hot and itchy under the wig, and he wanted to rip it from his head and scratch. The queue moved forward and he was at the desk. He handed the passport to the uniformed policeman.

"How long will you be staying in Hong Kong?"

"Only a few hours." He spoke in a hoarse whisper and coughed into a handful of tissues.

"A few hours?" The policeman looked at the passport more carefully. "You have come a long way for only a few hours."

"I am a business courier. I have to get papers signed and also supervise the transfer of funds."

The policeman stamped his passport, clipped the entry form to it and handed it back.

"I don't think I would like your job," he said with a faint smile.

"It's not bad. But I always seem to have a cold."

He walked through the barrier his heart pounding. Another hurdle overcome he thought, as he entered the customs hall. He pushed his way through the crowds of people waiting for their baggage at the conveyor belts. He approached the customs bench carrying his overnight case.

A young woman in uniform sauntered up to him.

"Is this your only case?" she asked, in a bored voice.

"Yes," he replied.

"Have you anything to declare?"

"No. Nothing."

"Please open it."

He fumbled with the clasp, the tissues in his hand making him clumsy.

"There you are," he said, opening the case wide. She swiftly felt inside.

"Thank you. That's all right."

He closed the case, lifted it from the bench and walked through into the main concourse of Kai Tak airport. He was immediately accosted by a tour tout brandishing leaflets, a representative from a hotel group with a clipboard and a porter wanting his case. He silently pushed his way through them until he was outside. The first blast of heat nearly choked him and he felt himself starting to pour with sweat. He recalled the aircraft captain's announcement just before they had landed. The temperature he had said, was 32^0C, and the humidity 93%. He removed the jacket of his grey suit

11

and carefully folding it, put it, together with his tie into his case. He opened his shirt at the neck and rolled up his sleeves as he approached a taxi.

"Star ferry, Kowloon," he said as he got in.

The traffic was bad and it was nearly twenty minutes before the taxi pulled up at the long approach to the ferry. He got out, paid the driver and waited until the taxi had driven off.

He turned away from the ferry entrance and walked swiftly up Canton Road, then right into Peking Road until he came to the main Nathan Road. He paused uncertainly then turning right he walked more slowly until he came to the Shui Hing department store.

He quickly ran his eye down the store guide and then he went to the third floor, grateful for the sudden air-conditioned chill. He went straight to the cutlery counter pulling out a wad of tissues from his trouser pocket.

A smiling assistant approached but he took no notice of her as he sniffed into the tissues he was holding to his face.

At last he pointed to a large carving knife and in a hoarse voice asked the price.

"34.95, but we have some more over here," she said starting to move away in the direction of another counter.

"No. That will do," he said pulling out a handful of coins.

He waited patiently until she brought him his change and gave him a neatly wrapped parcel. He left the store and walked back towards the ferry. A large electronic clock in a jeweller's window, caught his attention. The time was flashing — 12.08. He checked with his watch, 5.08, he was well up to time.

He stopped at a coffee shop and looked through the window. He saw what he wanted and went in. He sat at a table in the corner near the telephone on the wall. A waitress put a glass of water on the table and he ordered coffee and cheesecake. He waited until she had brought it and then he began to undo the parcel that he was holding on his knee, under the table.

He took the knife from the box, holding the tip of the blade with a bunch of tissues, and carefully eased it, handle first, into his right hand trouser pocket, stretching his leg as far as he could, to prevent it jabbing him. The box and paper he slipped into his case. It was an uncomfortable position but he sat like this until he had finished his coffee and after paying the bill, he stood up shaking his leg slightly as he went to the telephone. He kept his face to the wall as he dialled and waited for the ringing tone to be answered.

"Hello. Yes?"

His heart leapt. He knew he would be there, it had been arranged, but supposing he had not? There had always been that risk. He spoke in a hoarse voice, distorted by the pads in his mouth.

"Mr. Phillips?"

"Yes. Who's this?"

"I think you know who sent me."

There was a long pause.

"Are you Walker?"

"That's right."

"Well, what now?"

"Can we meet? I haven't got much time."

"Can't make it to-day. It'll have to be sometime to-morrow."

The telephone became slippery in his grasp.

"It has to be today. I have to be somewhere else to-morrow."

The urgency in his voice penetrated the hoarseness.

"Well, I'm going out now. In fact you only just caught me. How about this evening at 8 o'clock?"

He had to be half way to Bangkok by 8 o'clock. Better start pushing.

"Look Mr. Phillips. You wanted this meeting. I've

come a long way, and I want a meeting this afternoon otherwise I'll report back you wouldn't see me and you'll get nothing."

"Now look here. Don't start taking that line with me."

But there was a note of uncertainty in his bluster. He decided to press hard.

"2.30 at the Star ferry, Hong Kong side. The two telephone kiosks by the bookshop. Don't be late."

"Why there, for God's sake? and how will I recognise you?"

"Because I've been told to talk to you outside — minimise eavesdropping — both human and mechanical, and I'll know you. I've got a photograph."

He replaced the receiver before the other man had a chance to reply.

He looked at the clock on the coffee shop wall — 12.32. It could all be over in a little more than a couple of hours. He was well up to his timetable.

He walked out into the blinding sun and stifling heat. His clothes were sticking to him and he was feeling tired. He strolled slowly towards the ferry conscious of the knife in his pocket.

He paid the fare and went through the first class turnstiles. He walked down the long corridor following the crowds. The red light changed to green as he neared the gate, and it swung open allowing the mass of people to walk down the slope across the gangway and on to the top deck of the ferry.

He sat in the non-smoking cabin at the front deep in thought, until the bell signalling the closing of the gate made him once more aware of his surroundings.

He gazed at the skyline of the "World's Most Magnificent Harbour", as it started to come closer. Seven minutes later he stepped ashore on Hong Kong Island.

He hung back, walking very slowly, allowing the hundreds of passengers to move ahead of him. He was almost the last passenger to emerge from the corridor. He walked beyond the book shop, bearing away from the street down the smaller corridor that led to the harbour railings. Near the end in a small recess virtually hidden from sight were two telephone kiosks set into the stone wall. He went into the right-hand one in the corner and examined it carefully. He came out, strolled to the railings and looked back at where he had been, then walking back again, he passed the kiosks and looked over his shoulder at them.

He meandered up and down Des Voeux Road looking in the shop windows for over an hour. Then without hurrying he made his way back to the ferry entrance. A clock showed 2.10 as he turned right into the short corridor. When he reached the telephone kiosks he entered the one that he had examined previously and balancing his case on one knee he opened it and removed a pair of grey cotton gloves. He pulled them on and stood the case in the corner. He then took the knife from his pocket and put it on a ledge over the entrance to the kiosk.

Then leaning against the wall he picked up the telephone receiver and put it to his ear holding it in such a way that his hand half-obscured his face.

It was ten minutes later that he saw Phillips walking slowly and it seemed, carefully down the corridor and he wondered whether he had been drinking.

He turned towards the wall as Phillips approached and pretended to talk into the telephone. He felt Phillips behind him, then Phillips coughed and asked softly "Mr. Walker?"

He took no notice and felt him move away. Still holding the phone he slowly turned, his eyes quickly looking up and down the corridor. He listened carefully but he could only hear Phillips's footsteps as he ambled up the corridor.

"Mr. Phillips," he called, "over here."

Phillips turned in surprise and started walking back. "Why didn't you say who you were before?"

He half turned away still holding the phone and did not reply.

"Who are you talking to?" Phillips said belligerently as he came up to the kiosk.

"You'll soon know, he wants to talk to you."

"It's him?" Phillips asked incredulously, "on the phone? Now?"

He took the phone as it was handed to him and entered the kiosk as the other man moved out.

"Hello, hello." Phillips shouted. "Here, what's going on? This phone is . . ."

There was a clatter as the phone fell out of his hand. He tried to turn, his eyes bulging, but the other man had his knee in the small of Phillips's back and was pulling the thin wire tight around his neck.

Suddenly there was no resistance, and Phillips was dead. The other man had a little difficulty in removing the wire, so deeply had it become embedded in Phillips's neck.

He moved fast, constantly listening for approaching footsteps. Gripping Phillips under the shoulders he hoisted him to a standing position, and wedged the dead man's right shoulder and arm into the crevice in the corner of the kiosk. He stuck the phone into the left hand and closed the fingers around it. He bent the left arm and put the elbow into the corner of the ledge holding the directories, then rested Phillips's head on his left hand. He stepped back and looked. At a glance it seemed as though Phillips was in the middle of a long telephone call and had slumped wearily resting his head on his hand while he spoke. Only the legs were not too convincing.

He picked up his case and started to walk away, he had only gone a few steps when he remembered the knife still on the ledge. He turned to go back but then heard approaching footsteps. He hesitated for a moment, then continued walking towards the ferry. The knife had been for an emergency. In case Phillips had fought back. It could stay there. He took off his gloves as he walked and stuffed them into his trouser pocket and his fingers felt the loosely coiled wire. He worked the wire and the gloves into a tangled ball and as he passed the rail to the harbour he casually tossed the bundle into the water. He had never felt so exhausted in his life.

CHAPTER 2

Dr. James Firth was uneasy. He looked at his watch and then slowly lifted himself out of the chintz-covered armchair. The pain when he moved was quite bad this morning and he stood awkwardly for a moment waiting for it to subside. He looked through the big bay window at Lake Windermere and noticed that there were some boats already moving on the still water. He once more glanced at his watch trying to ignore the thinness of his wrist. Almost eight o'clock. By lunch the strain should be over.

"Good morning Doctor, did you have a good night?"

He turned painfully towards the door as his housekeeper came in with his breakfast on a tray.

"I've had worse, Nell."

"And how is our guest?"

"Still sleeping," he said sitting down at the table.

"Will I see him before he goes?" she said as she laid the table from the tray.

"Of course you will. Look Nell, it was nothing personal. He just wanted a couple of days without people and a long, uninterrupted sleep. And that's just what he's had."

The telephone rang as she was about to reply and she walked over to the armchair in which he had been sitting and picked up the telephone from the floor.

"Hello, Dr. Firth's house." She listened for a moment and then said, "just a moment please. I'll put Dr. Firth on."

She brought the telephone on its long lead to the table and putting it down next to the toast rack, said, "it's Number Ten Downing Street. They want to speak to the Prime Minister. It's urgent."

* * *

"This is bloody ridiculous," said the Rt. Honourable Peter Reid M.P. — Leader of the House of Commons and Deputy Prime Minister. He glared at the young man standing in front of him who appeared totally unmoved by the show of anger. Alan Wood was used to it. He had been Private Secretary to Reid for over four years and was not impressed by his employer's reactions when under pressure. In fact he had said more than once to his intimate friends that he hoped nothing ever happened to the P.M. whilst Reid was his deputy. He knew that really there was no such position as Deputy Prime Minister, but that had not stopped the last few Prime Ministers from appointing one. He looked at Reid slumped behind his desk, overweight, untidy and pouting with annoyance because the Prime Minister wasn't available to speak to him on the telephone, and some country doctor had told him so.

"When did he say he would be available?" Alan Wood asked.

"Sometime after lunch," Reid growled, then he added, his voice rising, "he's still asleep. Good God how much bloody sleep does one man need?"

"Can it wait?" Wood asked.

"I don't know," Reid replied thoughtfully, "it's a security matter and when those boys say it's important it usually is. Anyway I'll see if I can hold them until this afternoon, otherwise they'll just have to wake up the Prime Minister."

* * *

The Right Honourable Richard Driver M.P. Prime Minister of England was fighting to keep awake as he

19

drove the rented Ford up the M.6 towards the Lakes. He desperately needed a drink. Water — tea — coffee — anything. But he could not risk stopping and the possibility of recognition. He knew he was dehydrated from the long flight, confused by the jet lag and emotionally exhausted by what he had done. The monotonous motorway drive was dangerous in his present condition and he tried to keep the danger in the forefront of his mind. He looked again at the dashboard clock 10.15. If all went well he should be back by noon. He scratched his head then straightened the wig, pushing the large dark sun glasses further up his nose. The rubber pads tasted awful in his dry mouth but he had had to put them back into his mouth after a child had looked at him curiously from a passing car. She had not recognised him but he was not going to take any chances at this late stage.

The car was becoming unbearably hot and the cooling fan did not seem to be working. If only he could have a drink. That had been a bad oversight, it would have been easy to buy something at Heathrow Airport. He dismissed his carelessness as jet lag and tried to concentrate on the future.

But his mind kept drifting back to the last forty-eight hours, searching for any slips or mistakes which he may have made. The journey back had been uneventful, the only problem having been his tiredness. The flights had been on time and he realised yet again what a weak link that had been in the chain of events which he had created.

He made a conscious effort to bring his mind to the present and he hoped that Jimmy Firth had managed to hold everything together. Had he totally accepted the story that he had told him? And if he hadn't? Did it matter? How long did Firth say he had left? The Prime Minister had been shocked when he had seen him on Saturday. Was it now really only Tuesday morning?

He was so tired and so much had happened. But now he was free and clear. Wasn't he? Free and clear. The blaring horn of a passing lorry startled him and he quickly returned to his own lane realising that he had almost fallen asleep. He put his foot down and as the car picked up speed the Prime Minister briefly wondered why he didn't feel free and clear.

* * *

It was going to be a hot day, James Firth decided, as he gently lowered himself on to the garden seat near the boat house. He looked out over the lake marvelling at the different colours on the hills beyond. Mary had loved this spot and had sat there for hours knitting. He smiled wryly as he thought of the numerous occasions on which he had complained about the clicking needles, and wished for the thousandth time that he could hear them again.

He wondered what she would have made of all this. She would have probably patted him on the cheek and told him he was silly to get involved in cloak and dagger work at his time of life. His fingers absently stroked the cushion beside him on which she had so often sat. He wished he had not got involved. Not now. Not so near the end. He hadn't really wanted to but Dick had always been persuasive, persuasive and demanding, and after all he was Prime Minister. Funny that. He had always known he would go far. But Prime Minister? He supposed that everyone who really knew successful men felt like that. No — that was not quite true. Dick's achievement had been a surprise to everyone including Dick himself. It had been a compromise after numerous meetings and after the bitterness had set in, when none of the front runners would concede to each other. He had not really been in the running, hardly mentioned as even having an outside chance.

But it had happened, because he also suited the new party image. A businessman, self made, who would stimulate the economy and bring entrepreneurial skills to the governing of the country.

He had often wondered where Dick had got his first money. But that was part of the mystique. Early days confused. Never knew father. Mother died when he was seven years old, succession of institutions and then the year out East where, as he put it, "he learned about life." He had also obviously learned about money, James Firth mused, shifting slightly as a spasm of pain briefly suffused his body.

Returning to England on his twenty-first birthday he had within ten years made himself a millionaire several times over. Property development had been the basis of his fortune but then he had revealed a skill and tenacity in buying ailing companies and turning them into profit that had made him a glamour figure in the City. Politics had been a natural progression — a new world to conquer.

James Firth watched a power boat skimming across the Lake and remembered the first time he had met Richard Driver. He must have then been about twenty-five and just becoming known outside his immediate business circles. There had been a minor accident right outside the surgery in Hampstead and Driver had come in and asked for treatment for a cut hand. Firth remembered how charming Driver had been, joking about having accidents outside doctors' surgeries. Then Mary had come in with the tea, thinking surgery was over, and surprised to see Driver, had invited him to join them. It was during that tea that a mutual love of book collecting emerged and that the seeds of a deep and trusting friendship had been sown. Mary had always thought that Dick abused the friendship and that it was a relationship in which he had given and Dick had taken, and on looking back perhaps she was right. Although when Mary had died Dick had been a tower of strength. But then again when Dick's bride of a few months had been killed, it had been he and Mary who had seen the shattered young husband through his grief. And now this. He wished he knew more. But Dick had convinced him it was necessary for him to 'disappear' for two days without anyone knowing that he had done so. He had hinted at National Security, at an enormous international gamble and to be fair to him, had also acknowledged the magnitude of what he was asking. "Especially," he had said, "especially as we both know your state of health." Firth had got the message. If, whatever it was, went wrong, he would not be around to get into trouble. He reckoned he had another two or three months before the affairs of this world bothered him no more.

It was Dick's insistence on absolute secrecy that had worried him and still did so. Surely the security services or Dick's secretary or even that clown the Deputy Prime Minister should know, and what if he did not return, supposing there was an accident whilst he was away? What was he meant to tell people? "The truth, Jimmy," Dick had said. "Tell them the truth, and I'll leave a document somewhere that will clear you. But it will be unpleasant, I realise that."

In the end he had gone along with Dick as he knew he would. "Lamtons" had been perfect for the purpose. He and Mary had bought it many years before he had retired and they spent more and more time there in the two or three years preceding his retirement. Dick had often stayed with them over the years, and knew the routine well. It had been his plan as to how things were to be managed.

"We'll leak a story of my being overtired and that I'm going to stay with you at Lamtons for a few days of absolute and total rest," he had said. "Everyone knows you're a doctor, and although there's a risk of rumours starting that I'm not well, it's a risk I'm prepared to take. I'll come to you on a Friday or Saturday and then on Sunday and Monday you'll tell everyone I'm in bed and that you've given me something that will make me sleep for a long time," He had paused for a moment before continuing, "you'll have to think of something that will satisfy Conway." Conway was the Prime Minister's personal doctor and Firth had been expecting a call but so far none had come.

"What about Nell?" he had asked Dick, "she's going to know."

"No, she's not," Dick had said emphatically. "I'm afraid that's just another problem you're going to have to deal with. No one but you will know that I'm not in the guest room at Lamtons from early Sunday morning until Tuesday lunchtime."

"What about your special communications?" he had asked him, "the last time you stayed here as Prime Minister they put in a special red phone, and made a mess of the wall when they removed it after you'd gone."

"Leave that to me." he had said, making a note on his gold-edged pocket note pad. "I'll fix that somehow." He'd fix it Firth had discovered by installing Andy Blaine, his personal secretary, and all the equipment up the road at the Belsfield Hotel. Andy had told him there had been absolute hell from the communications section who wanted to know why. The other big hurdle that had been anticipated had been Dick's personal detective, Detective Inspector Arthur Wade, but in the event he had been reasonably happy with his bed in the boxroom and had so far spent his time sitting on the lawn reading his way through a pile of library books he had brought with him. "Never known such a peaceful two days since I've been with the P.M.," had been his only comment.

Firth looked at his watch — 11.30, should not be

long now before this whole charade was over. He pushed himself up from the seat and slowly made his way to the water's edge and stood leaning against the side of the Boat House.

The Boat House was small and white and at the corner of Lamtons lawn that went down to the lake. There was a thick hedge dividing Lamtons from the neighbouring property, running from the water's edge past the side of the Boat House up the garden along the side of the house to the road. There was a very narrow track between the hedge and wall and try as he might Dr. James Firth could see no movement behind the hedge.

* * *

The Prime Minister drove the rented Ford into the large carpark in Bowness at the edge of Lake Windermere. He put the key in the dashboard locker and got out of the car after checking in the driving mirror that his hair, glasses and pads were in place. Carrying the overnight case he walked slowly and stiffly to the nearby telephone kiosk. He had memorised the number from the sticker in the back window of the car.

"Hello, Ford Hire? This is Mr. Hutchinson, I rented a car from you last Saturday and paid a week in advance. Well I've just met some friends who have room in their car and are leaving now for Scotland, I'm afraid I've no time to return the car to you as they are already very late. So I've left the car in the Bowness car park by Windermere. Yes that's the one. Deduct from what you owe me the cost of collection. The key's in the locker. Fine, thank you very much, sorry for the trouble. Goodbye."

He stepped out of the telephone kiosk and felt that he could hardly move another step. He started to walk. It was only ten minutes to Lamtons, to that narrow track between the hedge and the wall.

Leaving the car was almost the last act, he thought, as he walked with shoulders hunched and head down. The deposit and any rebate would be returned to them 'address unknown', but that should not be too unusual during a busy holiday season.

He had rented the car on the Saturday evening just before they had closed, having arranged all the details on the phone. It was the first time he had used the handful of tissues and streaming cold routine and it had appeared to work. They certainly seemed glad to see him go. He had then parked the car on the car park ready for him to drive to London just after midnight.

It had been a good dummy run, getting out of the house with no one seeing him, changing in the Boat House and then slipping out on to the road through the small gate leading from the narrow track. Lamtons was set back from a bend in the road and it was easy to make sure that the road was clear both of pedestrians as well as of traffic.

He was now almost at the bend in the road. He casually looked behind him and saw that the road was clear. He slowed down until two oncoming cars had gone well past him, and then quickly opening the gate he stepped into the gloom of the narrow track. He pushed his way down, being careful not to get scratched by the overhanging hedge, until it finally gave way to the side wall of the Boat House. There was a door with a small pane of glass through which he looked before he opened the door and entered the Boat House.

He changed rapidly into the casual shirt, slacks and beach shoes he had left wrapped in a parcel in a dark corner and making another parcel of everything he had been wearing, including the wig and mouth pads he put it in the small overnight case and after carefully wiping it both inside and out, he pushed it underneath an old tarpaulin. He pocketed his wallet containing the pass-port and driving licence made out in the name of Brian Hutchinson and then he made his way over to the large window in the far wall of the Boat House. Looking through it he saw James Firth standing at the water's edge gazing out over the Lake and when he looked towards the house he saw his detective, Inspector Arthur Wade, sitting in a deck-chair outside the open french windows, reading a book. He looked back towards Firth, and then he gently tapped on the window. At first he thought that Firth had not heard him and he was just about to tap again, when Firth slowly straightened his shoulders and casually turned towards the Boat House. He knew by the expression on Firth's face that he could see him through the window and so he pointed, jabbing a finger towards the deck chair and the reading detective. Firth nodded almost imperceptibly and started to wander towards the house. He saw him say something to Wade, who smiled and then got out of the deck chair and followed Firth through the french windows and into the house.

The Prime Minister took a deep breath, opened the garden door of the Boat House and stepped out into the August sunshine.

* * *

Andrew Blaine, private secretary to the Prime Minister, had been relieved at the summons to go to Lamtons at once. The Prime Minister had sounded rather tired on the phone and had in fact joked that he felt more tired now than before his long sleep. "Must be something to do with the drugs Dr. Firth gave me," he said. This had surprised Blaine as it was the first time that drugs had been mentioned in connection with the Prime Minister's rest. Now watching him as he worked his way through the 'Urgent' files, Blaine

27

thought that the Prime Minister looked far from well. His eyes were sunken and black rimmed and there was an uncharacteristic pallor to his face. For the first time he thought he looked his age. His usual youthful appearance was a feature of the man and it was generally agreed that he looked ten years younger than his 49 years. Of medium height, slim and with unruly brown hair it was said that he brought out the maternal instinct in enough female voters for it to be a significant electoral factor.

"Fine, Andy, fine," he said, in the rich tones so beloved of impressionists, "there's nothing here that won't wait apart from this security flap. Tell Mr. Reid that I'll deal with it from here."

"What time do you want to leave in the morning?" Blaine asked, stuffing the files into his case. The Prime Minister looked at his watch, "I know this may upset a few plans but I'd like to go back to London to-night. See if you can arrange for us to leave about six."

"It's three o'clock now," Blaine said, inwardly fuming at the change of plan. The bloody man was so unpredictable, no thought for others, utterly selfish when it came to things like this and yet when he wanted to he could be unbelievably thoughtful and charming.

"Yes, I know," the P.M. said standing up, "so we'd better get moving."

Blaine picked up his case left the room and went in search of Arthur Wade. He found him in the kitchen having a cup of tea with the housekeeper.

"We're off at six," Blaine said sourly, letting his feelings show.

"Off where?" Nell Patterson asked.

"Back to London. The P.M.'s changed his mind. I'll tell the others at the hotel, and we'll be here ready to leave at six."

"What about supper? Will you have it before you go?"

"Damn," said Blaine. "I forgot to ask him. You know he doesn't bother about small things like meals."

"You can say that again," she said. "In the last forty-eight hours he's only had a bowl of fruit."

"Really," the detective said, "why was that?"

"Don't ask me. I think the Doctor must be . . ." She suddenly checked herself and flushed. "Anyway it's nothing to do with me if the Prime Minister wants to cut himself off from everybody. I mean to say, does it matter if I saw him unshaved and half-asleep — the vanity of some people."

"And not only politicians," Blaine said, "what about policemen who sit in the garden all day trying to get a tan?"

Arthur Wade grinned. Tall and burly was the description of him in a newspaper article and he rather liked it. Soft spoken and even-tempered he often seemed to be watching the constant activity around him with tolerant amusement.

"Why not make some sandwiches and coffee and we'll have them about five-thirty," he suggested mildly, "at least I will Nell, I don't really care about the others."

Nell laughed, her good humour restored by this large quiet man. "I'll think about it," she said, "but you better find out what the Prime Minister wants."

* * *

"Did it all work out as you wanted Dick?" Firth asked.

The Prime Minister glanced about him as he strolled in the garden with his host.

"Better than expected Jimmy. I'm only sorry I can't tell you about it."

Firth gave him a searching look and for a moment the Prime Minister was startled. Then Firth said, "I don't think I really want to know. By the way you took a chance just wandering into the house like that from the garden and asking where the hell everyone was."

The Prime Minister thought to himself that that was the least of the chances he had taken but he said, "I suppose I did. But listen Jimmy I want to thank you for everything and there's just one other small thing." Firth stiffened. "Relax," he smiled, "it's not a problem, but underneath that old tarpaulin in the Boat House you'll find a small overnight case. Do me a favour and burn it. The garden incinerator should do the trick."

Firth nodded wearily, "all right, I'll see to it to-morrow."

The Prime Minister put his arm around his old friend's shoulders and was surprised at how thin and frail he felt.

"Take care Jimmy, and remember if there's anything . . ."

"Will I see you again?" Firth interrupted not looking at him.

"Of course you will, there's the big shindig in Glasgow next month. I'll stop off on the way back."

* * *

The Prime Minister's party left Lamtons for London shortly after six o'clock. An hour later Nell tried to wake Dr. James Firth for his tea. For a moment she thought that he was dozing in the large chintz covered armchair, but then she realised that he was dead.

CHAPTER 3

Philip Melrose Vivian Potts, Potty to his staff, friends and acquaintances, was the editor of the Daily Globe. A tabloid newspaper with a circulation nudging three million, it was owned by Sir Hubert Dugdale who was described in numerous articles in other publications, as a maverick among millionaires, due to his left wing tendencies. He was also other than Potts' mother, the only person to call him Philip.

"I won't tell you where I heard it, Philip," he said looking his editor in the eye. "But you can take it from me it's worth investigating."

"How much do you think is involved?"

"Over three hundred thousand pounds." Dugdale said blowing smoke from his long Havana cigar towards the ceiling.

"Christ. How did he get in so deep?"

"That's for you to find out," Dugdale said briskly, standing up, "I'm sure you have ways and means."

Potts nodded slowly as he eased himself out of the red leather chair in his proprietor's large office.

As always he was conscious of his height or lack of it, when he was with Sir Hubert Dugdale and wondered what other people remarked when they saw them together. At well over six feet Dugdale towered over Potts, who although admitting publicly to being five feet, was always conscious of the missing inch and a half.

"By the way," Dugdale said, "I liked Shaw's piece today. Good strong stuff. Perhaps you'd let him know."

"Of course. He'll be delighted," Potts said as he left the office.

Dugdale grunted. He often wondered whether he should not send memos to his newspaper as many other proprietors did, but he preferred to send messages through the editor. He fancied it made him more remote and less open to the charges of interfering with policy. But of course he did interfere. As he had said to his wife on more than one occasion, "what's the point of owning a newspaper if you can't interfere?" She'd agreed. But then, she agreed with everyone and everything. That's why he'd married her. For that and the money.

He stood in front of the large window overlooking the park. He ran his 'affairs' as he described them, from a self-contained flat on two floors in Park Lane. On the ground floor were three rooms off the entrance hall, one was a waiting room and the other two were occupied by his secretary and a typist. Most of the first floor was taken up by his office, but there was still space for a bedroom, a tiny bathroom and toilet and a kitchenette with a bench and table. He spent two or three nights a week in the flat, his wife Lucy preferring to stay in the country at the cottage.

He walked away from the window and sat down behind the large rosewood desk. He picked up the blue telephone which was a direct line to the exchange, by-passing the three line board in the typist's office downstairs, and rapidly dialled a number.

"Paul? Hubert here. I've sent the ferrets in but I don't know if they will come up with anything." He listened for a moment than said, "of course I'll be discreet, but now it's out of my hands. As soon as I know anything I'll let you know." He replaced the receiver and looked at his watch. Four-thirty. He once again reached for the blue phone and dialled.

"Hello, Maxine? Are you free? About six-fifteen, the staff will have gone by then. Fine. I'll be waiting."

He sat back, his eyes involuntarily glancing at the

bedroom door. He knew he would feel better after an hour with Maxine, although he doubted whether she would feel as equally relaxed. He smiled as he thought of what was to come.

* * *

Philip Potts jabbed a key on the intercom and when his secretary answered told her to find Roger Shaw and tell him to come up before he left for the day. Ten minutes later there was a knock on the door and in response to Potts' growl, Roger Shaw walked into the editor's office, sat down in the chair in front of the desk and brought out a pipe and tobacco pouch from a side pocket of his safari style jacket.

"Must you?" Potts said getting up and opening a window.

Shaw grinned but didn't reply. Potts looked at him, enviously. Tall, handsome and always immaculately groomed, he was at thirty-three the heartthrob of the typing pool and beyond. He was also a fine reporter, Potts reflected as he searched for a suitable opening.

"Sir Hubert is very pleased with you. He thinks you're a good little boy and that your homework on the crooked chemists was very good."

"Can I have a raise?"

"Shut up. Now while he may think it was good, you and I both know that he knows nothing about journalism, so his opinion doesn't really count. Does it, Roger?" Potts asked.

"Of course not. You are the repository of all judgement and wisdom on the Globe," Shaw intoned mockingly.

"You'd better believe it," Potts said cheerfully. "Now then pay attention and listen. Peter Reid, Leader of the House and Deputy Prime Minister may be in debt to the tune of three hundred thousand pounds. I want you to prove it. I want to know how, why and to whom. I want facts, figures and dates and he's not got to get even a whiff of your scent."

Shaw puffed at his pipe but his eyes never left the other man's face.

"You discuss this with no one, it's not mentioned at the editorial conferences, and you report directly to me. O.K.?"

Shaw thought for a moment. "Any leads?"

"Nothing."

"Any hunches?"

Potts hesitated for a moment, then shook his head, "none."

"Where did you hear it?"

"Mind your own bloody business and go away."

Roger Shaw got up and stood to attention and looking straight ahead he said, "I wish to tender my resignation."

"Get out," Potts shouted, "before I accept it."

Roger Shaw grinned and left the room. Potts spoke into his intercom "no calls for ten minutes," and then laying back in his chair he swung his feet on to the desk and closed his eyes. He wanted to think this one through. He had tried in the car coming back from Dugdale but so far he was not satisfied. It smelled. Not the fact that Reid was in financial trouble, he had no high opinion of the Deputy Prime Minister, it was more the way Dugdale was going about it.

Potts did not particularly like the proprietor of the Globe but he was a good employer and on the whole he let him get on with his job of editing the paper without too much interference. It was no secret that Dugdale was politically Left wing, but in fairness to the man, Potts thought, he had not pushed the Globe too far in that direction. In fact the Labour Party had on occasion complained just as vigorously about the Globe as it had done about the so-called 'Rightwing Capitalist

Press'. But Potts had always considered Dugdale somewhat of an enigma. He had married money and invested it well. He had bought the Globe some eight years ago from the playboy son of its founder, and seemed satisfied enough providing it showed a nominal profit. In the few years that Potts had been his editor he had never really understood what Dugdale got out of owning the Globe. There were rumours of women in the Park Lane flat, but Potts had never heard of the Globe being used to provide them. But one never knew. There seemed to be an unending supply of 'starlets' and 'models' who wanted to see their photograph in a national newspaper.

Potts slipped further down in the chair, his thoughts returning to Dugdale's left wing views. It intrigued him. There had always been the occasional millionaire in the Socialist movement. Some had even risen to cabinet rank, but they had been politically ambitious, and Potts thought cynically, the Labour Party had provided an easier route to the top. He even remembered a millionaire who had given all his money away due to his Socialist beliefs. But Dugdale shunned active politics although he was on close personal terms with the labour hierarchy and as a proprietor of a daily newspaper he also met from time to time leaders of all parties and factions. His knighthood last year had come from the Conservative party, who doubtless thought it would do them no harm in next year's general election. But it appeared they had been wrong, if this Reid business was going to be for public consumption, and so far Dugdale had never ordered him to suppress anything. There had been the occasional skirmish in reporting items that might have adversely affected major advertisers, but they had never resulted in a major confrontation. Potts considered himself a reasonable man and so far Dugdale had not asked him for anything that he felt himself unable to give.

He would just have to wait and see, Potts thought opening his eyes and removing his feet from the desk. But his old newspaper-man's instinct told him that the next few weeks could be quite interesting.

* * *

"How can you let me wear the same thing time and time again?" Fiona Reid snapped as she reached behind her and zipped up her dress. Her husband sitting, slumped on the end of the bed looked at his wife, his fleshy jowls quivering. She gazed down at him contemptuously, "Oh for God's sake don't start crying."

"You don't understand," he said huskily, his voice a shadow of the hectoring tone heard from political platforms throughout the country. Then, making an effort to pull himself together, he said more firmly, "how many times do I have to tell you. We're ruined. I don't know where to get any more money. I owe a fortune and it's only a matter of time before it comes out and then I'm finished."

"You're finished now," she said. "Just look at you, fat, sixty and broke. I don't know why I bother."

She sat down at the dressing table and looked at herself in the mirror. Fifteen years younger than her husband, her red hair and high cheekboned face together with a slim but good figure, had provided much needed glamour to the political scene. She liked the attentions of the photographers and as her husband had progressed up the political ladder she had also enjoyed the flattering notice of the younger members of the party who obviously found it no hardship to be pleasant to the beautiful wife of a senior and important colleague. That was the reason she had stayed with her husband. The only reason, she supposed. He had been plump when they had married, but not fat as he was now. He was already 'an up and coming' man when they had met, and that is why she had married him. She was already thirty with two long 'affairs' behind her and he had been something of a catch. But now. Leader of the House, Deputy Prime Minister and just look at him. She still could not fully understand what had gone wrong, although he had explained it to her several times. She knew the position but she just could not understand how he had got into it.

"Why not go and see the P.M.? Maybe he could help."

"Don't be so bloody stupid," he replied glaring at her. "If he so much as had an inkling of the trouble I'm in he'd ditch me overnight. He never really wanted me in the first place."

"I can believe that," she murmured.

"Anyway," he went on, "why should anyone help. It's not as if I were P.M. I've no real patronage. I can't dish out peerages and knighthoods."

In spite of herself Fiona Reid laughed. "Oh come on, we're not living in the days of Lloyd George. You don't really think you could raise hundreds and thousands of pounds by selling honours."

"It's not done as obviously as that," he said with a touch of condescension, "these days it's all much more subtle."

"Well you're not P.M. so stop whining. Now get ready, the car will be here shortly."

"What's the point?" he replied.

"The point is that we're due at a diplomatic reception and that, for the moment anyway, you're the Deputy Prime Minister. So come on."

She watched him struggle to his feet and go into the bathroom. He looked worse than usual. What the hell was she going to do? Would the P.M. ditch him? She doubted it, not now only months away from an election. He could be a bastard, everyone knew that, but he was also a shrewd politician and he probably had ways of sorting out this mess. She thought of him as she smoothed the yellow silk dress over her thighs. He was always attentive when they were together, but not excessively so, and on more than one occasion she had caught him looking at her. He had never remarried, and since he had been Prime Minister he had been very careful with whom he had been seen, although the political grapevine was constantly busy with gossip. He would be at the reception to-night. Should she say anything, however obliquely? Her husband would have a coronary if he found out. But what was the alternative? Disgrace? Humiliation? And didn't she have a duty to the Party? To hell with the Party she had a duty to herself. She was sure that the last thing the Prime Minister wanted just now was a major scandal. She thought that in fact he would probably go to great lengths to cover one up.

*   *   *

Roger Shaw rubbed his eyes, yawned prodigiously and closed his notebook. He got up from the sofa and walked in stockinged feet to the kitchen and took a can of beer from the fridge. He looked with mild distaste at the mess in the sink and vowed to clear it up before he went to bed.

He enjoyed living alone, but missed having someone to clear up after him. His mother had pampered him when he was at home, and then his sister who had lived with him until she had married six months ago, had looked after him. The flat in Chelsea was really too big for one person and the cleaning had become a chore. But he owned it even if he could not really afford to have someone clean it. It had been left to him by his mother, who had owned it as an investment for over twenty-five years. Within eighteen months of his

38

mother's death the tenants had gone to live with their daughter in Australia, and he had moved in with his sister who had come to work in London.

He drank the beer out of the can, still enjoying the pleasure of doing so without his sister calling him a slob and making him use a glass.

He thought that he had the first glimmerings of truth regarding the tangled affairs of the Right Honourable Peter Reid, but he was a long way from getting the facts and figures wanted by his editor. He felt out of his depth in the complex financial scene and he wished he could call on the City Editor for help, but Potty had been quite adamant. No one else was to be brought in.

He thought over what little he had. Somehow or other Reid owed over a quarter of a million pounds, without ever having been in business. He didn't gamble and although Shaw bet that the lovely Fiona cost him plenty, their life style was not really extravagant. So where had it gone? As far as he could find out Reid lived off a few small investments and his Member of Parliament and Ministerial salary. He had entered the House of Commons at the age of thirty and before that he had been a teacher. When Dick Driver had become Prime Minister it had caused some eyebrows to be lifted when he had elevated Reid, then a junior member, into the cabinet. Two reshuffles later and Reid was Leader of the House and Deputy Prime Minister. The political commentators were full of conjecture, and talked knowingly of checks and balances within the cabinet, and Reid had got on with the job with, as someone had written, 'uninspired competence'.

Roger Shaw was startled when the front door bell rang. He glanced quickly at his watch and saw that it was nearly midnight. He walked to the door, looked through the spy-hole and then swiftly opened the door.

"Anne," he said, his face wreathed in a smile, "I thought you were in South Africa. Come in."

The trim blonde in the uniform of a British Airways stewardess moved into his open arms as she kicked the door closed behind her.

"Why didn't you phone or something?" he said picking up her case and leading her, one arm around her waist, into the lounge.

"No time," she laughed, pleased by the warmth of his welcome, "but I'm glad you're in. Couldn't face another hotel room. It's all been absolute chaos. That's why I haven't been in touch. Quite frankly darling, I don't really know what day it is. I'm completely zonked. They've moved the schedules around so much that no one knows where they are, never mind where they are meant to be."

"You're staying?" he asked hopefully.

"You bet," she said starting to take off her uniform. "But first I'd like a long hot bath and a large cool whisky."

"So where have you been?" he asked moving towards the tray of drinks.

"Mainly on the Hong Kong run," she said, "and that's why we're so late today."

She took the glass of whisky from him and sat down on a low foot stool in front of the sofa wearing only her briefs.

"You'll catch cold," he said looking down at her fondly.

"You can warm me up later," she said in a theatrically seductive voice.

He laughed as he pulled her to her feet. She was fun, open and uncomplicated.

"It was weird," she said suddenly.

"What was?"

"I was telling you the reason we were late taking off from Hong Kong. I mean, what was I meant to say to the passengers over the speakers? 'British Airways regret this delay in departure due to the late arrival of a coffin containing an Englishman murdered here in Hong Kong six weeks ago. We hope you have a pleasant flight and thank you for flying British Airways.' "

Roger Shaw laughed uncertainly. "What are you babbling about? You really are zonked."

"No, I'm not," she said draining the last of the whisky, "the purser told me. The guy was called Albert Phillips and he was found strangled in a phone box in Hong Kong near the ferry, and you know what Roger? The murderer had fixed him in such a way so that he looked as if he was on the phone. Isn't that creepy?"

"Creepy," he agreed.

"Anyway, it seems that Phillips had left a note or something saying that if there was enough money left after he died, he wanted to be buried in England."

"Have they caught the murderer?"

"Not yet, and they probably never will. Murder's two a penny in Hong Kong, and the police have their hands full. But Jack said . . ."

"Who's Jack?"

"The purser. He said that they were taking more interest in this case than they would normally have done because the murdered man was a bit of a boozer and when he was sloshed, he used to boast about his powerful friends in the Government."

"The Hong Kong Government?"

"No the one here.. But he was a drunk, so it's all probably rubbish."

Roger Shaw propelled her towards the bathroom.

"Enough of this gruesome talk. Go and have your bath and don't fall asleep."

"Well, it's interesting isn't it?" she pouted.

"Very" he said thoughtfully, "very interesting indeed."

CHAPTER 4

From Downing Street itself No. 10 appears to be a house of modest proportions, but at the back, connected to it by a long passage is a much larger house which stands in a large garden and looks across Horse Guards Parade. On the first floor of this part of the building are the beautiful state rooms which are situated above the Cabinet Room on the floor below.

The Prime Minister liked the Blue Drawing room best, with its Chippendale furniture, the Romney portraits around the blue papered walls and the Morland over the fireplace. The Waterford glass chandelier was ablaze as he sat in the corner of the sofa, facing Jake Boyle who was sitting on the edge of a matching sofa, a clipboard in his hand and an earnest expression on his face. All the paraphernalia of television lay around them as Boyle said, "as we near the end of this wide-ranging interview, Prime Minister, I wonder if I may turn to a more personal matter."

The Prime Minister waited, as his interviewer rearranged his features into an expression of concern.

"I refer to your health," Boyle continued, "and I must say looking at you today, here in Downing Street, you appear, if I may say so, to be in better health than I have seen you for some time. However, you must be aware of the concern that was expressed some six or seven weeks ago, when you were in Cumbria on holiday and appeared to be out of action for a few days."

The Prime Minister chuckled. "It's the old story, Jake, if my opponents can't defeat me in the ballot box or in the House of Commons, they try to do it by smears and innuendos. But as you say, your're here, you can see for yourself, it's all nonsense. However," he said becoming grave, "as you will also know my host and close friend the late Dr. Firth passed away at that time and naturally I was affected."

Jake Boyle whilst nodding sympathetically debated swiftly whether he should point out that Dr. Firth had died after the Prime Minister had left. But he decided to move on.

"Prime Minister, it is mandatory upon you to call a General Election before the end of next year. Would I be right in thinking that in view of the present apparently healthy state of the economy that it is likely you will do so, sooner than some people may think?" Boyle looked at the Prime Minister expectantly, his face reflecting innocence.

"Really Jake, you don't honestly expect an answer to that one do you?"

"Honestly, no" Boyle grinned, "an answer yes."

The Prime Minister gave an exaggerated sigh, then catching sight out of the corner of his eye, of a signal to Boyle, indicating that the programme was nearly finished, he suddenly became serious as he launched into his final answer.

"The question is not one of expediency. Obviously, I — that is we, would like and indeed will, win the next election. But that election will not take place on the urging of the media or for some short term political advantage. No, it will take place when this government, which has, I must remind you, a strong working majority, decides that it has carried out this phase of its work, and that this country is in a position both at home and overseas, to take advantage of the great opportunities that lay before us. Only then will we ask the country for a further mandate."

"Prime Minister, thank you," and turning so that he looked directly into one of the cameras, Boyle continued, "that's all from 'Viewpoint', this week. Join us next week when we shall be back in the more mundane

43

environment of the studio. Till then from No. 10 Downing Street. Good night."

As the red light went out on the camera, a buzz of conversation broke out as tensions were released. The Prime Minister stood as a young woman unclipped the microphone from his tie and disentangled him from its cable. Boyle approached him.

"Thank you very much, that was good."

"Good for whom, you or me," the Prime Minister said smiling.

"Oh we win some, we lose some, I think that one was about even," Boyle said accepting a drink from the tray being offered. They looked at each other for a moment, like old sparring partners then simultaneously they burst out laughing.

"Why do we do it, Jake? Answer me that, why?"

"Because it's important. People have a right to know what's going on."

"Balls. Most of them couldn't give a damn."

Boyle was surprised. The Prime Minister was not often given to this sort of talk. As if sensing Boyle's reaction, the Prime Minister said, "it's the end of a long day, and I've still got two boxes to do."

Boyle put out his hand. "Thanks once again, I look forward to the next time."

The Prime Minister shook Boyle's hand and clasped his shoulder in the timeless politician's manner and giving a cheery wave left the room.

It had gone well, he thought as he walked down the corridor to his study, especially that question as to his health. He wondered however, whether he should have mentioned Jimmy Firth. It looked as if he was using a dead man for sympathy, and even though he was, it looked bad.

*　*　*

44

Jake Boyle saw Andrew Blaine about to follow the Prime Minister out of the room. The Prime Minister's secretary turned as Boyle reached him.

"Hello Jake. Good interview."

"Thanks Andy. But I wonder if you could just clear up that business in the Lakes? Off the record of course."

"There's nothing to clear up, on or off the record," Blaine said sharply. "You heard what he said. It's a load of nonsense."

"Oh come on Andy. No one sleeps for five days especially Prime Ministers."

"It was two days not . . ." Blaine stopped and reddened as he realised the trap he had fallen into. "He was in touch of course," he continued lamely.

"Whilst he was asleep? That's a good trick Andy." Blaine turned on his heel and Jake Boyle watched him as he walked down the corridor to the Prime Minister's study.

"What did happen up there in the Lakes?" Boyle muttered as he turned back into the room, he really must try and find out.

* * *

The Prime Minister sat in the white tweed armchair in the first floor study of No. 10 Downing Street. A bright cheerful room with modern furniture and modern paintings on the walls it was in sharp contrast to the state rooms on the same floor. He did most of his work in this room, leaving the flat upstairs for total relaxation. At least that was the theory. But today he felt tired, and he was beginning to feel a reaction to the television interview earlier that evening. He pressed the remote control panel on the arm of his chair and watched the television set in the corner come to life. He changed stations until he found the News Programme he was looking for. The news reader paused before starting a new item.

"Earlier this evening in a television interview, the Prime Minister, the Right Honourable Richard Driver, refused to speculate on the timing of the General Election. He said his government would complete its work before seeking a further mandate. In response to a question about his health, the Prime Minister dismissed the rumours as being 'political smears and innuendos.'

The Prime Minister watched without hearing as the news went on, and he wondered what would have happened if he had truthfully answered the question about his 'illness' in the Lakes. He was still rather ashamed at the relief he had felt when arriving back in London he had been told of Jimmy Firth's death. He had counted on it of course, but not so suddenly. It had been a few hours before he began to worry about the overnight case under the tarpaulin in the Boat House. Firth had been going to burn it the following morning. The funeral had been in London, so he had had no reason or opportunity of returning to Lamtons and attempting to recover it.

He had decided after a lot of thought to leave it alone. The chances were that it would be thrown out with all the other rubbish when the Boat House was eventually cleared out. He had heard that under the terms of Firth's will, Nell Patterson the housekeeper, could stay at Lamtons for as long as it took her to find other accommodation, and when he had spoken to her at the funeral she had not appeared to be in any hurry to move on. So, he had reasoned, it could be some time before the case was discovered, if ever it was, and even then there was absolutely nothing to connect it with him.

"If only," he thought turning off the television, "if only they would forget about his two days' indispo-

46

sition, then he would be clear."

Robert Conway, the Prime Minister's doctor had tried to discover what Firth had given him, and had in fact telephoned Lamtons shortly after Firth had been found. But he could tell his doctor nothing, and after a severe lecture on the absolute necessity of checking with Conway before he took any medication from anyone, Conway had let the matter drop, suavely turning aside the questions from the press.

The telephone on the glass topped table by the chair rang and the Prime Minister answered it.

"Mrs. Reid for you, Sir."

"Mrs. Fiona Reid?" he asked with surprise.

"Yes Sir."

"Put her on."

"Hello, Prime Minister, I know it's late and I'm sorry to bother you."

"That's all right Fiona, it's always a pleasure to talk to you at any time."

"Yes, well, thank you, but you see it's Peter."

"What about Peter?"

"He's just tried to kill himself."

* * *

Arthur Wade the Prime Minister's detective had the door open before the car had stopped and followed the Prime Minister as he hurried into the side entrance of the hospital. They were met by a silver-haired man wearing a pin striped dark blue suit.

"I'm Dr. Mathis, we spoke on the phone." The Prime Minister shook hands with him and as they started to walk down a long brightly lit corridor he leant towards him and asked in a low voice, "how is he now?"

"Better than when he was admitted, but we're not out of the wood yet."

47

"You told Mrs. Reid I was coming?"

"Yes, and she's most grateful."

"Press?"

"Not yet, but there's bound to be a leak, especially now that you are here." As if confirming the doctor's words, the Prime Minister became conscious of turned heads and whispered words of recognition. "Say nothing at all, make no statements, neither confirm or deny anything, and perhaps you could ask the hospital spokesman to contact and then liaise with Don Parrish my press secretary."

"Certainly Sir."

The Prime Minister turned to Arthur Wade who was following a few steps behind them.

"Arthur, arrange for twenty-four hour security outside Mr. Reid's room, and make sure that they know what they're doing. Unobtrusive, but very firm."

The detective nodded as he reached into his pocket for his radio.

"Here we are Sir," Mathis said as he turned into a short passage off the main corridor. "This will only be a temporary room, but it's more private than most." He opened the door and stood back to let the Prime Minister enter.

Reid was laying on his back, arms by his side, wrists bandaged, with a tube from a bottle suspended above his head, attached to his right arm. His face was ashen and his eyes were closed. Fiona Reid looked up from the bedside chair in which she was sitting as the Prime Minister entered.

He went to her and holding both her hands in his, noticed how cold they felt in the hot and sticky room.

"Are you all right Fiona?"

"I — I think so," she said, her voice unusually high and her lips quivering.

He noticed that she had been crying, even though she had obviously made up her face and done her hair.

48

Her metallic blue dress was cut low and he was very aware of her figure. He turned to Dr. Mathis, who was talking quietly with one of the two nurses in the room.

"Is there anywhere we could talk for a few minutes?"

"I'm sure the Administrator would not mind you using his office. He's not likely to want it at half past one in the morning."

He led the way and the Prime Minister and Fiona Reid followed. It was only a few doors down the main corridor and finally they were alone in an ultra modern office.

"Well now," he said smiling gently as she stood looking at him, "let's first of all make ourselves comfortable."

He sat down in one of four black chairs clustered round a table, and motioned her into another.

She sat down and crossed her legs. "I tried to tell you the other night," and seeing his puzzled look, she added "at the reception. I tried to tell you, but I didn't think you'd understood."

He remembered the conversation. He'd thought she'd been flirting with him as she'd talked about her husband in enigmatic terms.

"I'm sorry I didn't realise . . ."

"I know. It's not your fault. It's mine. I should have told you or someone ages ago, and maybe it wouldn't have come to this." She waved an arm vaguely.

"Well tell me now."

"It's money. We're broke, and Peter owes a fortune."

"How much?" he asked, astonished at what she had said.

"As far as I can make out it's well over a quarter of a million pounds."

He was stunned. "How on earth, I mean I always thought of you both as . . ."

She laughed mirthlessly at his confusion.

"Oh, we've not spent it. Peter's lost it."

Part of the Prime Minister's mind started to assess the political implications as he listened. He knew things had been going too well and his calvinistic streak had been waiting for some calamity. But this would be a scandal in which his opponents would revel.

"It's the end isn't it?" She asked looking at him intently. "You've got to sack him. You can't cover this one up. Can you ?"

For a moment his stomach contracted at her words until he realised she did not mean what he thought she'd meant.

"First things first, Fiona. Tell me exactly what the position is."

"I don't know exactly. That's the trouble. Peter's told me several times in general terms, but that's all I know."

"Well," he said with a hint of asperity of which his staff were well aware.

She looked at him sharply and said, "yes you're quite right I must pull myself together." She took a deep breath and the squaring of her shoulders thrust forward her breasts. He waited and pointedly looked at his watch.

"He was taken for a ride by a con man," she began, "I suppose that's the best way to describe it. I knew nothing about it until a few months ago. But apparently it all began over eight years ago. Peter met this man who convinced him that he could make a fortune in some overseas mining operations. Peter told him that he had no money, but the man said that with Peter's contacts surely he could raise some. I don't know how, but apparently he did. I think it was while he was a Junior Minister at the Treasury he met some Swiss gnome who put him in touch, in return for a favour with some other overseas Banker and it was all done under nominees and things like that. Of course interest had to be paid on the money, but they said he could, what's the term, 'roll it up'. And as far as I can see that's what happened. It rolled itself up to tens of thousands of pounds and although the initial amount was quite a lot, the high interest rates have made it astronomical. Peter kept pestering this man as to when the deal would be completed until it slowly dawned on him that there never had been a deal.

"The silly thing," she went on, "is that we really didn't need the money. But Peter knew he'd never succeed you and that he'd only got where he was, because it enabled you to control the Party, and that you considered him safe and no threat." She stopped him as he started to protest. "That's all right, whatever else Peter was — is — he's a realist. He just wanted to make sure he had something for his old age. He said he'd seen enough has-been politicians living off their House of Lords' attendance money, and he didn't want to end up like them."

"What was this man's reason for approaching Peter in the first place?"

"Oh he said something about needing someone in high places to sort everything out once the deal had been completed, otherwise it would all go in tax. I forget the exact reason but it seemed plausible to Peter at the time. And of course having met the man through you, he thought he could trust him."

"Through me?" The Prime Minister said with surprise.

"Yes. Apparently he was with you at the Party Conference in Blackpool many years ago and he kept in touch with Peter after that. The trouble was of course, that he was living in Hong Kong and it was always difficult to get hold of him."

She looked curiously at the Prime Minister as the colour slowly drained from his face.

CHAPTER 5

"I'd go to him pretty sharpish, if I were you son, he's been asking for you all day."

Roger Shaw grinned at Stan Bowlder custodian of the desk in the entrance hall of the Globe building just off Fleet Street. Bowlder had started with the Globe as a messenger boy, and apart from war service, had been with the paper all his life. Known throughout Fleet Street as Stan of the Globe, he had seen numerous editors come and go but referred to them all as Him. His habit of gazing upwards whilst saying the word had confused more than one young reporter.

"Maybe he wants to make me deputy editor," Shaw said as he strolled towards the lift.

"If he does I'm off," Stan called after him.

Shaw took the lift to the third floor, walked down the corridor and entered the office of the editor's secretary. Stella Fish, had been with Potts for over ten years, and had moved with him when he had changed jobs as he climbed the Fleet Street ladder. She was in her late fifties with a motherly manner and her protection of Potts was legendary. He in turn trusted her implicitly.

"He's not very pleased with you," she said seriously as Shaw entered her office.

"Why?" he said unsmilingly, he didn't trifle with her when she was in this mood.

She did not reply, but spoke into the intercom on the desk. "Roger Shaw's here."

"About bloody time, send him in."

Shaw walked through into the editor's office.

"Where the hell have you been?" Potts shouted glaring at him from behind his desk, and before Shaw could reply, he went on, "I gave you a job to do on

Reid. Since then the silly prick tries to kill himself, and you've buggered off."

Roger Shaw sat down in the chair in front of the desk and pulled his pipe from his pocket. This seemed to enrage Potts even further, "if you light that bloody thing, I'm warning you I'll throw both you and it out of this office." He stood behind his desk challenging Shaw like a fighting bantam cock.

"I've been to a funeral in Liverpool," Shaw said quietly.

"Whose funeral?" Potts asked warily, his anger visibly subsiding.

"One Albert Phillips."

"Who is he? A relation?"

"No, I never knew him, and I'm not too sure who he was."

"Go on," Potts said menacingly, "and it better be good."

"Last month, Monday August the eighth to be precise," Shaw said pulling a notebook from his pocket, "a body was discovered in a phone booth in Hong Kong . . ."

"Hong Kong," Potts shouted, "Hong — bloody — Kong. What's that got to do with anything?"

Shaw continued as if there had been no interruption. "It was identified as being that of Albert Phillips, an Englishman, aged about fifty, who had been living in Hong Kong for about seven or eight years. He had the beginnings of a drink problem, and when drunk would talk about his powerful friends in the British Government."

Potts leaned forward his previous scowl replaced by a look of interest.

"He had no business and apart from referring vaguely to his 'deals', he had no obvious source of income," Shaw continued. "He lived with a Chinese woman in a reasonable flat but by no means in the best part of the Island. I haven't been able to find out what he did before he went to Hong Kong, so I thought I would go to his funeral."

"In Liverpool?"

"Yes. He left instructions that if there was enough money he wanted to be buried in England, in Liverpool."

"Why?"

"I don't know."

Potts sat back in his chair and looked thoughtfully at Shaw, "go on."

"Who said there's any more?" Shaw said lighting his pipe.

"There had better be."

"Well, I'm not sure, and I can't prove it yet, but I think Reid knew Phillips."

"How close are you, to proving it?"

"I could do with some help."

"What sort of help?"

"The financial editor."

Potts thought for a moment and then said, "I'll think about it and let you know. In the meantime stick with it."

Shaw got up and Potts said, all traces of his previous anger gone, "and in future, bloody well keep in touch."

When Shaw had left the room Potts asked Stella Fish to get the proprietor, Sir Hubert Dugdale, on the phone.

* * *

The Right Honourable Paul Jowett M.P., Leader of the Opposition, stirred his tea as he read the report, in the early edition of the evening paper, of the Deputy Prime Minister's attempted suicide. It said that Reid was 'stable', and Jowett hoped that he would not die. He had been shocked when he had been told the news early that morning and his first thought was that Reid's action was in some way connected with the 'tip-off' he had given Dugdale about Reid's financial affairs. He had immediately telephoned the newspaper owner and Dugdale had assured him that Reid would not have even known of the investigation. He had said he would ring back after he had spoken to the editor, but when he had done so, it had been only to say that they could not contact the reporter assigned to the story. He had promised to telephone Jowett as soon as he had any firm news.

"Are you in, this evening?" his wife asked, coming into the sitting-room from the kitchen of the small Westminster flat.

"Yes, I think so, but it depends if anything further blows up over this Reid business," he said.

"Do you know why he did it?" she asked sitting down next to him on the large overstuffed sofa.

"No, but Hubert's working on it."

She wrinkled her nose in distaste. "Do you have to have anything to do with him?"

He laughed and put his arm around her. "He's very useful and we need all the help we can get, especially in the next twelve months."

She pulled away from him and got up. "Why don't you retire gracefully, Paul?" she said looking down at him, "you can take a peerage, and still be involved."

"Not now, Molly," he said gently "don't let's go through it all again."

He watched her as she picked up the cup and saucer from the arm of the sofa and walked back into the kitchen. He knew she hated London and this flat, with the division bell that rang whenever there was a vote taking place in the House of Commons enabling him to be there within four minutes.

He also knew that if he lost the forthcoming election the party, facing possibly five years in opposition, would force him at sixty-two to make way for a younger man. Molly would be delighted, he thought wryly. All she wanted, was to be a full time grandmother and spoil their three grand-children, away from the glare of publicity. He realised that she was bored with politics and all that went with it. However, he knew that she loved him, and in the end, would go along with whatever he decided to do.

The trouble, he acknowledged to himself, was that he was not at all certain what he wanted to do. He recognised that he did not possess the ruthless ambition that conventional wisdom said was necessary to get to the top. But he also knew that he owed his present position more to seniority and compromise, than to outstanding ability. He had fought and lost one election as Leader of the Party and only survived because of the interminable squabbling amongst any of the possible usurpers of his position.

Perhaps Molly was right. Why push it? Retire with dignity and honour and watch the rest of the circus from the front circle. He freely admitted that he was tired of the political juggling and tight-rope walking and he felt that his outlook would not materially alter even if he was elected ringmaster. So why go on? Vanity he supposed. The ringing of the telephone startled him.

"Hello. Oh hello Hubert," he said and then he listened without commenting for some time. "Thank you very much. Your people have done a good job as far as it goes. But let me know as soon as you hear anything definite. Thank you again Hubert. Goodbye."

He lay back in the sofa, his mind digesting what he had just been told, and concluding that politically it could be rather dirty. He wondered however, whether he had the will or even the desire to use it for his own political ends. He decided not to discuss it with Molly — and immediately he felt ashamed.

The security service opens a file on every Member of Parliament as soon as he is elected. It is amended where necessary, as further facts are received through normal channels as well as from information that is actively sought by D.I.5 itself, as an M.P. progresses up the parliamentary ladder and reaches those positions that require security clearance.

Sir John Meeling, head of D.I.5, which used to be called M.I.5, and is responsible for internal security, closed the red coloured file with the blue label, on which was typed the name 'Peter Reid M.P.'

"A bit thin isn't it Sir John?" the Home Secretary said.

The security chief nodded, and waited for Henry Winterbottom to continue. The Home Secretary's responsibility for D.I.5 was the reason Sir John was sitting in his room at the Home Office waiting for the florid politician to get to the point.

"Do you, that is — ," the Home Secretary was always nervous when talking to the security people, and even though he knew his own file was blameless, he felt as he did when he went through customs with nothing to declare. "Is there anything further you know, that isn't in the file?" he said to the moustached, tall figure with the military bearing sitting opposite him.

"Nothing significant," Meeling said in his clipped manner.

"Well, what do you make of it?"

"Difficult to say at this stage, could be money. Unlikely to be women."

"Why is that?" The Home Secretary leaned forward, eyes gleaming with curiosity, "he's not a . . ."

The head of D.I.5 let the politician flounder. "I mean, is he a homosexual?" he finally muttered not looking at the other man.

"No. Nothing like that. It's just that we'd probably know if he was busy with women. Word gets out. Financial dealings are a different matter, we usually only hear about those when something goes wrong."

"I see. Well I suppose you'll continue to search for the reason?"

"Yes."

"Have you spoken to Mrs. Reid yet?"

"No we haven't, but the police have and she told them that she has no idea why her husband tried to kill himself." Meeling paused for a moment and then said, "I was wondering if perhaps he was in some political trouble that had got out of proportion."

"Good God no. Not that I know of. Anyway politicians never kill themselves over political crises," the Home Secretary chuckled, "otherwise there would hardly be any of us left."

"Just so," Sir John Meeling said, with but the faintest trace of irony.

"Well thank you for coming and putting me in the picture," the Home Secretary said, "and please keep me informed. You see," he leant forward confidingly, "you see the Prime Minister is naturally taking a very close interest indeed in this matter and asked me to let him know at once, if you uncover anything."

"Most understandable," said the security chief, as he got to his feet.

* * *

Maxine Lambert pulled the front door of Sir Hubert Dugdale's Park Lane flat closed behind her and walked slowly and stiffly towards Marble Arch.

She would have to give up this type of client she decided as she shifted her bag from one painful shoulder to the other. They paid well, in fact they paid very well, but one day one of them would go too far and she would be maimed for life.

Dugdale was getting worse, she thought as she started looking for a taxi, and something had certainly excited him earlier tonight. He had had a glitter in his eye when she had arrived and he had carried on long after she had really told him to stop.

She wondered whether it was anything to do with the telephone call he had received. He had taken it in the room next to the bedroom and had not fully closed the door. She had heard snatches of the conversation and could tell they were talking about the Reid affair. Dugdale had then made another call and he had done all the talking, his voice rising in his excitement. She had been surprised at what she heard, but then he had returned and she had concentrated on the bedside clock, ticking away the remaining minutes of the hour of her life which he had bought.

CHAPTER 6

The Prime Minister let the newspaper slide off the bed and join the mass of other papers already on the floor.

He poured another cup of coffee from the silver coffee pot, added cream from the small silver jug, and settled the breakfast tray more comfortably over his knees as he sat, three pillows at his back in bed. He picked up 'The List' from the tray. It was a plain white card on which were listed his appointments for the day. As the day wore on it was altered as unexpected crises and pressures surfaced. But his life was ruled by it and copies were given to his secretaries, drivers, and bodyguards and to his assistants who fought for unscheduled minutes during which they could influence or promote their own particular projects.

Further copies of 'The List' were to be found in the study and cabinet room, and a very small pocket version was prepared for the Prime Minister to carry with him during the day.

He glanced at the digital alarm clock radio on his bedside table, 7.36, he then looked at the first entry on 'The List' — '8.00 Parrish'.

He knew what Parrish wanted. A statement. It was over twenty-four hours since Peter Reid had slashed his wrists and so far there had been as one of this morning's papers had put it, 'a deafening silence from Downing Street'. Last night he had promised his Press Secretary Don Parrish a statement first thing this morning. Parrish had wanted one last night that would appear in the morning papers and had been annoyed at the delay.

The Prime Minister had been rocked by what Fiona

Reid had told him and for the first time since his return from Hong Kong felt a small but gnawing worry in the pit of his stomach.

He had returned to Downing Street from the hospital and had slept badly. Yesterday had been a busy day which required him to concentrate on detail, with the Party Conference due in two weeks followed by the reassembling of Parliament after the summer recess. But his concentration had faltered, and it had showed.

He got out of bed and padded barefooted into the adjoining bathroom. He washed his face, cleaned his teeth, combed his hair and went back into the bedroom and climbed back into bed. He had a long hard day ahead, and he had, from the very first days of becoming Premier, realised the necessity of pacing himself throughout the day.

He looked again at 'The List', mentally ticking off what would be required from him at each appointment. He enjoyed the challenge of each new problem, seeing them, although he would never admit it publicly, as weeds in a beautiful garden, that had to be removed before they spread. He was a first class administrator, even his enemies granted him that, but he felt himself to have a vision of the future and a capability of implementing it, which he saw in no other senior member of either party. He had been surprised when he had been elected, but he had also been conscious, deep within himself, of how right the decision had been. He had quickly mastered the levers of power and was proud of his growing reputation overseas, culminating in a recent article in Time which had referred to him as a 'young statesman newly arrived on the world scene.' With youth on his side, he saw himself as at only the beginning of a career as a major world figure, and he openly enjoyed his contact with other leaders. He had been fortunate in establishing an immediate rapport with Wesley Sloane the new American President and still got pleasure from being on first name terms with him.

The bedside telephone rang and a secretary told him that his Press Secretary was waiting.

"Ask him to come up," he said, staightening the pillows and reaching for a thick pad of the blue paper on which he liked writing.

"Good morning Prime Minister," Parrish said as he knocked and entered. "Did you have a quiet night?"

"Very quiet Don, but by the look on your face it's not going to be a very quiet day. Sit down."

Don Parrish sat down carefully in a straight backed chair near the bed. He hitched his trousers with the razor sharp creases, crossed his legs, and looked expectantly at the Prime Minister.

"Stop looking at me like that."

"Like what, Prime Minister?"

"Like someone who is waiting for an apology, because you're not getting one."

Parrish laughed. He had met Richard Driver when he had interviewed him after a big business deal had been announced. Their paths had crossed as Driver had first of all entered politics and then started to rise. Parrish had been deputy editor with a news magazine when Driver had been elected Prime Minister and had asked him to become his Press Secretary.

Parrish had always liked Driver and knew he was susceptible to the charm that the Prime Minister could switch on whenever it suited his purpose. It had been switched on this morning.

"I see you've read them," Parrish said, stirring the jumbled newspapers on the floor with the toe of a highly polished shoe.

The Prime Minister looked at the tall superbly tailored, almost languid figure of Don Parrish and knew that behind the smooth manner was a very sharp mind.

"I've seen them and they were predictable."

"Predictable. Yes. But if I may say so, avoidable."

"You may say so," the Prime Minister said with a half-smile as he doodled on the blue pad. Then he suddenly looked up and said, "what's the latest on Peter Reid, have you heard how he is this morning?"

"A slight improvement, but it's still too early to say."

The Prime Minister nodded and sat up straighter in the bed.

"A deafening silence," he said quietly, "but I've really nothing to say other than expressions of deep regret. I don't know why he did it. Have you heard anything?"

"Only more explicit rumours of the ones published today."

The Prime Minister snorted, "they've hinted at everything from espionage to call girls. It's disgusting while he's lying critically ill in hospital."

"Maybe if they had a statement," Parrish ventured.

"All right. You've made your point. Draft something on the lines of 'deep regret, overwork, pressure of high office, nation's prayers with him and family at this time, and end with a hope that he and his wife will be left in peace and privacy in their time of trial."

Don Parrish reached into the inside pocket of his dark blue jacket and produced a neatly folded piece of paper. He leant over and handed it to the Prime Minister, who unfolded it, read it and who then burst out laughing. "You old bugger," he said handing the paper back, "that's perfect, issue it now."

"It won't hold them for long," Parrish said.

"Look Don. Let's get our priorities right. This will be a nine days' wonder and I want it played down from the start."

"It's a big story and I've had calls from all over the world, it will have to blow itself out, I'm afraid. It's far too big for me to kill."

"Well keep me informed, but I want to maintain a low profile on this one."

"What about Mrs. Reid?"

"What about her?" the Prime Minister said, instantly regretting the sharpness in his voice.

"Do you want me to deal with the press on her behalf? I understand she's already somewhat besieged even though she's made it quite clear she has nothing to say."

"Yes Don, that's a very good idea. See what you can do otherwise you don't know what they could trick her into saying under pressure."

* * *

Fiona Reid opened her eyes and tried to establish the cause of the metallic clicking that seemed to be coming from the small white armchair in the corner of the bedroom. Then she remembered that she had taken the receiver off the telephone and stuffed them both underneath the seat cushion of the chair. The Post Office must be putting the noise down the line, which they did to attract attention when they thought the receiver had been incorrectly replaced.

She stretched her body under the floral pink sheets and closed her eyes. She did not want to get up and face another day like the one she had had yesterday. She wondered if the photographers and reporters were still grouped outside the house. She had silenced the telephone after finding that nearly every call was from either the press, radio or television.

It suddenly occurred to her that perhaps the hospital might have been trying to contact her. She got out of bed, the white silk pyjamas with the vivid red sash blending with the white and gold furniture and furnishings.

She pulled the telephone from the chair and jiggled the hook until the clicking was replaced by the dialling tone. She dialled the number of the hospital as she carried the phone on its long lead to the bed.

"Hello? Dr. Mathis please, this is Mrs. Fiona Reid. What? Oh thank you. You're very kind." She had been surprised at the public's reaction to what she had considered to be her husband's folly and she was touched by the telephonist's brief words of sympathy.

"Dr. Mathis? Good morning. How is he today? She listened, sitting on the end of the bed as the doctor talked. "Well that's good. Thank you very much I'll be there in about an hour." She replaced the receiver and lay back on top of the bed. She had resisted those who wanted her to stay at the hospital overnight, as she wanted to get away from the appraising looks and speculative glances that she was conscious of receiving from the staff. She was also weary of maintaining her pose of bewildered grief.

He was going to live. The silly fool. But they were finished now. Both of them. The Prime Minister had not said as much in so many words, but she knew the political penalty for bringing scandal to the party — especially when it was in power. She sat up and traced her finger idly over the design on the eiderdown.

The Prime Minister had behaved strangely after she had said that it was Phillips who had been responsible for the trouble. She had noticed how pale he had gone and she had wondered why. Was it no more than that he was now connected with this mess, though remotely? Or was it something else? Her instincts had always been sharp and reliable and she was more than surprised when he had insisted that for the time being she must tell no one — and he had been emphatic on that — no one, about the reasons which lay behind the attempted suicide. He had seemed distraught and uncertain when he had left her and she had not heard from him since.

She slowly got off the bed and walked towards the bedroom window. She looked through the crack in the curtains and saw that the press were still there. She shuddered as she realised that she would soon have to go through that mob on her way to the hospital. She went to the front door and picked up the newspapers from the floor. She glanced at them as she walked into the kitchen and saw that she and her husband were front page news. She plugged in the kettle and sat at the counter waiting for it to boil. She extracted 'The Globe' because it was easier to handle and laid it on the counter. She quickly read about the 'Reid Sensation' as it was referred to, at one point smiling sadly at one of the wilder conjectures. As she reached over to turn off the kettle her sleeve caught the side of the newspaper and flipped it open at page five. Her eye was caught by a name that seemed to leap out of the page, 'Albert Phillips'. Her hands trembled as she read the report of the funeral in Liverpool of a man who had been murdered in Hong Kong but who had wanted to be buried at home.

Her first thought was that she should telephone the Prime Minister, but then she remembered that he read all the papers, and must therefore have seen the news.

She was still staring at the newspaper, when the telephone rang. She reached for the kitchen extension that was on the wall beside the counter.

"Mrs. Reid please," a woman's voice inquired. She was about to replace the phone thinking it was yet another press enquiry when the voice went on, "Number 10 Downing Street, here, the Prime Minister would like to speak with Mrs. Reid."

"Yes I'm Mrs. Reid."

"One moment please, I have the Prime Minister for you."

"Hello, Fiona? How are you this morning?" the rich

firm tones of the Prime Minister enquired.

"I think that the suitable phrase would be 'as well as can be expected,' " she replied.

"Good. Well keep battling on, and the reason that I'm phoning, other than to find out how you are, is to tell you that Don Parrish, you know my Press Secretary — is coming over to deal with any problem you may have in that direction. I suppose you do have problems?" he asked drily.

"If you mean do I have a crowd at the front door, the answer is yes." She waited for him to mention Phillip's funeral, the real reason, she was sure, for his call.

"Don's a good man, you can rely on him, and if there's any other way in which you think I can help, don't hesitate to let me know."

She realised he was about to hang up. "You have seen the papers this morning?" she asked quickly.

"I have indeed, but just ignore them. It will all soon die down, don't let them upset you."

"I meant, the — the — other matter," she said carefully and deliberately.

"What other matter?" the Prime Minister said with a touch of impatience.

She realised that he had not seen the item, probably because he only skimmed through the papers, concentrating on the political and financial news.

"Do you have 'The Globe' there?" she said quietly. She heard a loud rustling as a pile of papers was disturbed.

"Yes, I've got it."

"Look at page five, half way down the right hand side."

Moments later she heard a sharp intake of breath and Fiona Reed knew that her instincts had not been wrong.

* * *

Peter Reid opened his eyes and found it difficult to identify the person who was sitting at his bedside. He blinked several times and his wife slowly came into focus.

"Peter? Can you hear me?"

He tried to answer, but his mouth was dry and he found it difficult to move his lips. He looked at his wife as she bent over him a resigned expression on her face and he knew that nothing had changed.

"I'm sorry," he finally managed to croak.

She touched him lightly on the cheek, and said, "don't worry everything's going to be all right."

He felt a solitary tear well in his right eye and roll slowly down his cheek. He watched as his wife quickly turned away, but not before he had seen the scorn on her face.

He saw her say something to the nurse, the only other person in the room, who after a moment's hesitation nodded and went out, closing the door softly behind her. His wife was again bending over him.

"Listen Peter. Can you understand me?" she said a note of urgency in her voice.

"Yes," he said, so softly that she barely heard him.

"As I said everything's going to be all right. You've been a silly boy, but I'm going to make it right." She seemed as embarrassed as he was surprised by her motherly tone.

"Now, it's very important that you don't give a reason for what you did. Say nothing, do you understand?" She didn't wait for a reply but went on. "There's more to this than either you or I realised and if I'm to have any chance of rescuing something from this mess, you've got to leave everything to me. Now promise me Peter, you won't say anything to anybody and that includes the P.M."

He wanted to ask her so many things but he felt too tired, too hopeless, with an overwhelming feeling of desolation, that totally engulfed him.

"Do you hear me?" she said fiercely as the nurse re-entered the room.

"Yes, I hear you," he murmured, his eyes closing, and moments later he was asleep.

CHAPTER 7

"So you see Roger, it's very, very, complicated, no wonder you couldn't unravel it, in fact, I'm still not too sure of the finer points myself." Edgar Fowler, City Editor of the Globe beamed over his half glasses at Roger Shaw, who was writing in a notebook balanced on his knee.

"Do you understand it now, or would you like me to go through it again?" Fowler asked, as Shaw finished writing.

"I've got the general idea," Shaw said, "enough for what I need. At this stage all I was concerned with, was establishing a link between Reid and Phillips and there's now no doubt about that."

"None whatsoever. However, proving it, in say a court of law, wouldn't be all that easy."

"Why?"

"Because of the type of operator we're dealing with here would keep his mouth closed in any formal investigation and would be difficult to physically find if the heat was really on."

"And Phillips is dead."

"Exactly. By the way, you're not trying to link his murder with Reid are you?" Fowler asked as he lit a small dark cigar from the stub of the one he was smoking. The City Editor's office was thick with the smoke from his cigars as well as that issuing from the pipe clenched between Roger Shaw's teeth.

"I wasn't," Shaw said in reply to Fowler's question.

"So where do you go from here?"

"To Potty, I suppose, it's his decision or Dugdale's, to decide what to do with what I've got."

"Who did Potty get the original tip from?" Fowler

asked.

"He won't tell me, but I imagine it was Dugdale. I know he's leaning on Potty over this one."

"I see," Fowler said slowly, "well in that case my bet would be Jowett. Our proprietor is very thick with Her Majesty's Leader of the Opposition."

"How could Jowett have heard?"

"Ah, now then Roger," Fowler said beaming more than ever, "I can think of several of our overseas friends, even some that we've been discussing, who would profit from a nice, juicy, governmental scandal, and it wouldn't do Jowett's lot any harm either."

"We're getting into deep water," Shaw said.

"And very murky water, very murky water indeed," the City Editor said cheerfully.

Roger Shaw thanked Edgar Fowler for his help and leaving the office, walked thoughtfully down the corridor leading to the Editor's office.

"Stella my love," he said as he entered her office, "do you think you could arrange an audience — as soon as possible."

"That's no way to talk," she said with mock severity, "anyway he's got Sir Hubert with him just now."

"Sir Hubert Dugdale, here?" It was well known that the proprietor rarely visited the premises of the Globe, and that it was the Editor who had to go to the Park Lane office for meetings with him.

"Well, well," Shaw said, "the mountain has come to . . ."

"Stop it," she commanded, laughingly as she visualised the very tall proprietor.

Shaw turned as the door to the editor's office opened and he saw framed in the doorway Sir Hubert Dugdale looming over Philip Potts. He looked at Stella Fish and winked as she fought for control.

"Is there anything wrong Stella?" Potts said as he entered the office followed by Dugdale.

71

"I seem to have got something caught in my throat," she spluttered wiping her eyes. "I was sucking a sweet," she added, managing to regain her composure. Potts looked at her suspiciously then walking over to Shaw said to Dugdale "this is Roger Shaw."

"Delighted to meet you, young man, I've been hearing good things about you."

Potts scowled at Shaw as if defying Shaw to believe that the good things had come from him.

"That's very kind of you, Sir. It's most encouraging to know that I'm giving satisfaction." He thought Potts was going to explode.

"Tell me," Dugdale said, "how's your work on the Reid affair progressing?"

"As a matter of fact, that's why I'm here," Shaw said half turning so as to include Potts, "I feel I've made quite a lot of progress."

Dugdale looked at his watch, "I think I'd also like to hear your report," and he turned and strode back into the editor's office followed by the other two men.

"Let's have it," Potts said, sitting down behind his desk and motioning Shaw into the chair next to that in which Dugdale was settling his large frame. "Was Fowler any help?"

"Enormous help," Shaw said opening his notebook, "although I don't pretend to understand every twist and turn."

"Is there a connection between Phillips and Reid?" Dugdale asked, looking intently at Shaw as if he could see into his mind.

Shaw felt uncomfortable under his gaze, and concentrated on his notes.

"We've confirmed that Reid is in debt," he began, "and as far as we can establish he owes in excess of a quarter of a million pounds."

"Who does he owe?" Potts asked.

"That's where it becomes rather tortuous. You see it

all happened abroad, and it's only because of Mr. Fowler's contacts in Switzerland that we've managed to get anywhere,"

"Go on."

"Several years ago, a rather shady Swiss financier lent Reid a large sum of money so that Reid could participate in a mining venture in South Africa. He lent it without security and through a network of nominees on the strength of documents that Reid showed him and because of Reid's reputation on the British political scene."

"Without security?" Dugdale said with surprise.

"I understand," Shaw said referring to his notes, "that the money was lent personally to Reid at a rather high rate of interest and that he was to be personally liable for it by guarantee, even though the lender would require twenty-five per cent of any profit on the deal in addition to the repayment of his loan and interest."

"Were there any profits?" Potts asked.

"Not only was there no profit," Shaw said, "there was no deal. The documents were false and the contact who had set the whole thing up, and I guess, who had also pocketed the money, had all but disappeared."

"Phillips?" Dugdale asked enquiringly.

"Phillips," Shaw confirmed, and went on, "Reid was in a cleft stick. The interest was snowballing at a compound rate on his loan, and he had exhausted all his delaying tactics regarding repayments. He couldn't go after Phillips for fear of the ensuing publicity and scandal. At the best he would come out of it a gullible fool and at the worst as a bit of a rogue who mixed with shady financial characters, either way he would have been finished."

"To say nothing of the numerous Exchange Control Regulations he must have broken at that time," Dugdale said with satisfaction.

"He must have realised that there was no way out,"

Shaw continued, "so he tried to take his own life."

There was a silence when Shaw finished broken by Potts who said, almost to himself, "I wonder whether he knew that Phillips had been murdered, and was afraid that the investigation that would follow, would reveal his connection."

"How did you put all this together?" Dugdale asked Shaw curiously.

"When the news of Reid's attempted suicide broke, the Swiss chap realised he'd lost his money and told Mr. Fowler's contact enough for us to piece the rest together. Also I'd had a hunch about Phillips and that helped to point Mr. Fowler in the right direction."

"Do you think Reid had Phillips killed when he realised he was ruined?" Dugdale asked.

Shaw felt strangely repelled at the tremor of excitement in the proprietor's voice and the glitter that had appeared in his eye, it was almost as if he was getting sensual pleasure from the possibility.

"I've no reason to think so," was all he said.

"Phillips was a con man," Potts said, "this won't have been his only operation, there could be several people who would like to have seen him dead."

"What do the Hong Kong police think?" Dugdale said, "do we know?"

"I spoke to our stringer out there," Shaw said, "and I gather from him, that they more or less consider the case as just another unsolved murder. It appeared motiveless and he rather gathered that the authorities were not exactly broken hearted at the death of Phillips. They'd suspected him of several things from drugs to fraud but had never been able to prove anything. All they could find out was that he'd gone to meet someone in response to a telephone call and was never seen alive again."

"We've not got enough to go with yet," Potts said standing up and starting to pace around the office, "we

need some sort of statement of admission from someone, otherwise we'd have a writ on the morning of publication."

"How about seeing Mrs. Reid?" Dugdale said, "she
may know something."

Potts looked at Dugdale with annoyance, making it
clear that he did not need advice from his employer.
Dugdale remained impassive, and Shaw kept silent.

Potts stopped his pacing and sat down behind his
desk.

"I want you to see the Reids, him as well as her,"
Potts held up a hand as Shaw started to protest. "I
know it's going to be difficult, but that's what your're
paid for. Reid's on the mend and he's going to leave
hospital sooner or later, once he's at home you can get
to him. Also I want more on Phillips. Background,
associates, other business ventures etc., especially
before he went to Hong Kong. Then I want a statement. A Swiss gnome, Mrs. Reid, an accomplice, associates, informed girl friend, anyone who knows all or a
good part of the story." Potts waited for Shaw to finish
making his notes, and then said, "I would also like to
know how much Downing Street knows, but above
all," Potts said gazing at the far wall of his office, "I
would like to know how and through whom Phillips
first met Reid."

* * *

Paul Jowett lay in bed unable to sleep, his wife gently
snoring by his side.

The Leader of the Opposition was thinking about
the phone call he had received from Hubert Dugdale
earlier that evening. He felt that part of his inability to
sleep was due to his uneasy anxiety regarding Dugdale.
In some indefinable way he felt threatened by the man.
He was not too sure of what he was after, although he

75

suspected that he wanted to be the power behind the throne, "and," Jowett muttered wryly, "that is why he is so anxious for me to win the next election."

His wife stirred, and he became aware that he had given voice to his thoughts.

He was a political realist and knew that Dugdale would want something in return for his help, if Jowett won. He was not as far as he could judge, seeking political office or even further personal honour, although Jowett doubted whether Dugdale would refuse a peerage if it was offered to him. So Dugdale must feel that he could strongly influence Jowett, and achieve power through the back door. And, Jowett admitted to himself, he was probably right. He found that as time went on he had less and less stomach for the smearing and jostling and often worse, that was necessary in politics.

He envied the Prime Minister. He couldn't imagine Driver laying awake full of doubt and anxiety. He had always known what he had wanted and he had gone out and got it. He was, Jowett admitted to himself, a good Prime Minister and even his political opponents had more than a sneaking admiration for him. If any one man could win the next election for his party, that man was Dick Driver, Jowett reflected. He doubted whether the Reid affair would prove to be more than a temporary embarrassment, in spite of Dugdale's excitement on the phone this evening. Driver's party had always been good at closing ranks and papering over the cracks in a time of emergency. Not like his own party who seemed to delight in tearing itself apart in public every few years. Jowett sighed and turned over, as he realised how much of his time had been spent over the last few months just attempting to weld the party together in time for the election.

His only hope of winning, he thought forlornly, was if something happened to Driver, although he did not wish him any harm. Not that any harm would come to him — the bloody man was indestructable.

CHAPTER 8

"Our polls are showing you further ahead in personal popularity at the start of the final year of a parliament than any Prime Minister in the last twenty-five years."

Ray Fulton looked expectantly at the Prime Minister and was mildly disappointed at his apparent lack of interest.

"When were they conducted? Before or after the Reid business?" the Prime Minister asked the Secretary of the Party who was sitting opposite to him in the Downing Street study.

"We had started on the day the news broke, and we continued for a further two days."

"So you finished a week ago."

"That's right. They're bang up to date."

The Prime Minister doodled on the blue pad which was balanced on his knee as he sat in the white tweed armchair. He suddenly realised he had drawn an H intertwined with a K and he hurriedly scribbled over them. "What else?"

"I know how tight your time is, especially as you've got the Washington trip to prepare for . . ."

"By the way Ray, I've managed to postpone it for four days."

The significance of the Prime Minister's remark escaped Fulton for the moment, but then he laughed. "Jowett won't like that."

The Prime Minister grinned. The American President had gone along with the postponement, and if he had realised that the visit would now exactly coincide with Jowett's Party Conference he had not said anything. But it ensured that the Prime Minister would be in the limelight as an international statesman while Jowett was wrestling with party problems.

"However," Fulton went on, "I hope you can find time for the new candidates, they're anxious for some of your popularity to rub off on to them."

"Split them into regional groups, and see if you can fit in a couple of meetings here before the conference and I'll see the rest at Blackpool."

"That about clears it up then," Fulton said, stuffing papers into the attache case on the carpet by his feet. He was pleased with the last hour and a half as he knew that once parliament reassembled after the conference it would be more difficult to get the Leader of the Party on his own.

And to Ray Fulton, Dick Driver was more the Leader of the Party than the Prime Minister.

He drank the glass of whisky on the table beside him and got up.

"You won't forget to let me have something on Reid?" Fulton said, "I must know how you want it played. A lot of questions are being asked." He fancied the Prime Minister had become more alert.

"Leave it with me, I'll see you get something within the next couple of days."

After Fulton had gone, he walked out of the first floor study and climbed the nearby staircase to the flat on the second floor. He walked in to his bedroom and took off his jacket and shoes. He slipped into the old blue silk dressing gown he had been given over twenty years ago, together with the matching slippers and went into the sitting room.

The rooms in the flat had low ceilings and apart from the sitting room he found them rather oppressive. There were five bedrooms, four of them with adjoining bathrooms, a music room, dining room, sitting room and kitchen. He had turned the music room into a library for part of his rare book collection, even though it was still called the music room. The flat was too big for him and he rarely had people to stay. He preferred his own but small exclusive home in North London which he had designed for bachelor living, but the security people had persuaded him to live 'over the shop'. He felt lonely this evening and the knowledge that he had only to lift the phone, to fill the flat with people somehow made him feel even lonelier. He briefly considered making what he personally termed, one of his 'discreet phone calls, but he knew that tonight the answer did not lie in that direction either. Although he had built up friendships with several women whom he had found over the years to be trustworthy, and who would invite him to their homes for 'dinner', he was always aware of the risk to his image, even though they were all, outwardly at least, highly respectable ladies from good families.

The press constantly speculated on his private life but always came to the conclusion that he intended to remain faithful to the memory of his wife of a few months, who was tragically killed so soon after their marriage.

He had found himself thinking of Penny more during the last few weeks that he had done for many years. He had been happy with her, but wondered now if they would have survived as a couple, the pressures of a high-powered political and public life. But what he questioned most was whether or not he would have gone to Hong Kong and done what he had done, if she was still alive. Deep in his heart however, he knew that he would have done exactly the same. In fact there would have been in some strange way, a greater motivation. Maybe now he could consider marriage, which he had always dismissed whilst Phillips was alive.

He turned on the television as the News was starting, and watched as Fiona Reid helped her husband down the hospital steps and into a car. He noticed Don Parrish vainly attempting to curb the more enthusiastic members of the press who had gathered in force for this event. He watched the remainder of the mid-evening news and after turning it off he sat back and turned his mind to the Reids.

Fulton had wanted to know what line to take and so had several members of the cabinet in individual calls to him. He was grateful that Parliament was not sitting otherwise he would not have been able to stall as long as he had. He accepted that he had been stalling, and had been working on the principle of when in doubt do nothing. But he could not stall much longer.

Fiona Reid had phoned twice over the last two days and he had not returned either call. He remembered only too well the last time they had spoken, when she had pointed out the report of Phillips's funeral, and he had temporarily lost his composure. It was not surprising he thought, that he had been stunned. That Phillips, even dead, should turn up in England was not something he had bargained for.

He had felt that Fiona Reid had noticed his reaction and he had not felt himself able to talk with her since, but he could not put it off forever. On impulse, he picked up the phone and told the operator to get him Mrs. Reid.

When the phone rang he took a deep breath before answering.

"Hello Fiona. I'm sorry not to have rung you before but you know how it is. One damn thing after another."

He listened as she said that she understood, then he went on, "I saw you both on the news this evening, how's Peter?" She told him that he was in bed, weakened by the journey home and that there was a nurse with him. She asked if she could see him as soon as possible.

"Can you come over now?" He regretted the words

the minute he had said them, but he did not know why. He put the phone down after she had said she would be with him within the hour.

He went into the bedroom and changed into dark blue slacks with a pale blue sweater, he then went to his desk in the sitting room and worked his way through a stack of files finding it difficult to concentrate.

It was almost an hour and a half before she arrived but she did not apologise. He was aware that she had taken considerable care over her appearance. When she removed her coat, she was wearing a short blue, summer dress cut low both at the back as well as at the front, and every strand of her red hair was in place. She chose to sit on the long sofa and there was a flash of tanned thighs as she crossed her legs.

He thought that under other circumstances he could well have enjoyed her visit, but now he felt threatened, mentally as well as physically.

He looked at her, as she sat in his favourite armchair and he realised that she was nervous and that there was a growing tension in the room. It was broken by the ringing of the phone.

"Who? No, not now," he said, "and unless it's an emergency I don't want to be disturbed. I'll let you know when I'm free." He put the phone down and she said, "thank you, that was most thoughtful."

He shrugged dismissively. She looked around the sitting room and said, "it's very nice, but don't you get lonely?"

"Sometimes."

"Is that why you asked me to come tonight?"

He felt the anger welling inside him even as he recognised the sliver of truth in her remark. His voice was icy when he said, "I returned your calls. You wanted to see me. Remember?"

"Please," she said holding up her hand, "I didn't mean to be rude or upset you."

He did not reply, but waited for her to continue.

"Look," she started, "I'm not here to plead for Peter or anything like that, but we've got to decide what we're going to say and do."

He nodded in agreement but still kept silent.

"Don Parrish has been marvellous over the last few days but sooner or later someone's got to say something. The press can be most persistent, you know that, especially the Globe."

"Why the Globe in particular?" he said.

"They have a reporter called Roger Shaw, who has been pestering me in spite of Don. He even tried to get into Peter's room at the hospital to speak to him."

"Some of them can be very aggravating," he said sympathetically.

"And then of course, there's Peter's future. People are asking me whether he is resigning or if he has been sacked, and there is a limit to how long I can go on saying 'no comment.'"

"What does Peter say?"

"Nothing. He has hardly said a word all week. He just stays in bed or sits in his chair. He doesn't look at the television and he won't read the newspapers."

"He can't continue in office, you do realise that," he said softly.

She blinked rapidly two or three times, but did not reply.

"I think an immediate resignation on the grounds of ill health would be the best way. Don't you?"

"The best way for whom?" she said, matching his low tone. "What is to become of us? We owe a huge sum of money, and no one will offer Peter any sort of job after this. So what are we going to do?"

"Oh come on now, Fiona, it's not as black as all that,"

"Isn't it?" she said bitterly.

"Now look," he said briskly, trying to change the

83

mood, "you're an attractive woman who . . ."

"Who can what?" she suddenly flared, interrupting him, "go on the streets? Is that what you're suggesting? What am I worth Dick? Go on tell me. How much should I charge? Remember I've got to make a few hundred thousand pounds," she laughed mirthlessly with a note of hysteria entering her voice, "I'm going to be a very busy girl aren't I? Aren't I?" she repeated more calmly, her anger subsiding as quickly as it had arisen.

He waited a few moments until she had regained more control of herself and then said firmly, "I was going to say that you are an attractive woman with a fine mind and I'm sure we'll be able to fix you up with something. The money is a separate issue."

"Not to us, it isn't," she said.

"Is there nothing left?"

"Nothing. You see although the original loan was only secured by a personal guarantee, when the interest started to mount, Peter sold our investments and got a mortgage on the house in order to pay off some of the interest with the money. So you see, we won't even have a roof over our heads." She looked down at her hands, and said very quietly, "then I really will be on the streets."

"Now listen," he said, and he waited until she lifted her head and looked at him. "As far as the debt is concerned, it's unlikely that they'll press for it." He smiled at her look of surprise and went on, "there would be little point. If you've no assets, they'll just write it off as a bad debt, it wouldn't make any commercial sense to spend further money on trying to recover something that doesn't exist. Right?" She nodded. "The mortgage can probably be renegotiated to take account of the change of circumstances and in any case I may be able to help there, I still have contacts in the property business. Now as to the income position." She was looking at him with interest. "I'm not suggesting Peter resigns from the Commons, only from the Government. There has to be an election within the year, so in any event, I don't particularly want a bye-election just now. No. All that would happen is that Peter would give up his Ministerial duties, remain an M.P. for the remainder of this parliament and that will give you both time to decide on the future."

He sat back, feeling that he had done a good job in restoring her morale as well as having dealt with the immediate political problem. He was totally unprepared for the venom in her voice when she said, "you really are an arrogant bastard. You sit there disposing of people's lives as if they were used paper handkerchiefs. Just who the hell do you think you are? I've watched you over the years, smiling, charming, and as ruthless as they come. Nothing must stand in the way of the great Dick Driver. Friends, colleagues, you think you can charm them all, while you're climbing all over them. Well I've got news for your, Mister Prime Minister, you can't charm me." She got up and went and stood in front of his chair, legs astride, hands on hips, her face filled with fury as she looked down at him. "We're in this mess because of you," she shouted, "it was through you that Peter met Phillips. So don't think that we're just going to quietly fade away, broken and ruined, while you carry on ever upwards. Oh, no, you're in this as much as we are, and if you don't help, I'll talk." She turned away and walked over to the window.

He leapt to his feet, strode over to the window and spun her around by her arm.

"I've been very patient, Fiona," he spat out not concealing his anger, "but I've had enough. I don't know what you think you have to say when you talk, but don't you dare try to threaten me. I've tried to be sympathetic, I've tried to help. You're obviously overwrought and I am trying to remember that you're under a great deal of strain. I suggest that you go home, think over what I have said and when you're in a more reasonable frame of mind we can talk again."

They were standing close together as they faced each other and in spite of his anger and growing fear he was aware of her body in the revealing summer dress and conscious of the perfume that she was wearing. As if sensing his feelings she leaned slightly towards him, but her eyes became hard when he turned on his heel and walked away.

"I'll never be in a more reasonable frame of mind than I am at this moment," she snapped, "because if we can't work something out now, then I'm afraid I'll just have to take matters into my own hands."

He was standing near the door. "What do you want?"

"Some money and a peerage for Peter," she said promptly, "that way we can survive with a little dignity."

He opened the door of the sitting-room, "goodnight Fiona."

She looked at him disbelievingly, "is that all you have to say?"

"That's all."

She picked up her coat and handbag and without looking at him, swept from the room.

He walked over to the telephone, lifted the receiver and said, "I'm free now."

They were not, he thought, the most appropriate words under the circumstances.

CHAPTER 9

The Home Secretary could not remember when he had last been so happy. It was the unexpectedness of the summons to Number ten Downing Street that had made the surprise that much greater. Of course he had speculated as they all had done, as to who would succeed Reid as Deputy Prime Minister and what form any Cabinet reshuffle would take, but everyone had assumed that it would be some time before Reid actually went and the new man was appointed. No one had thought it would happen before the Conference and the general concensus of opinion had favoured the return of the Prime Minister from America as the most likely date for the announcement. But the Prime Minister had fooled them all. Henry Winterbottom thought happily as he stood at a window of his room at the Home Office.

"We can't go into conference in disarray," the Prime Minister had said, "and also I want a functioning deputy whilst I'm in Washington." He had then offered him the post of Deputy Prime Minister, explaining that for the rest of this Parliament, the Chancellor of the Duchy of Lancaster could also shoulder the duties of Leader of the House, thus saving any actual reshuffling of jobs.

He wondered how the rest of the Cabinet would take his appointment. He had jumped two or three places in the pecking order, although it was never too clearly defined in the party. He fancied though, that neither the Chancellor of the Exchequer nor the Foreign Secretary were going to be all that pleased. But Driver was a Prime Minister who could act from a position of strength. He was popular in the party as well as in the country and his fast rise to the top had meant that he had few, if any, long standing favours to repay.

The Home Secretary frowned as unbidden to his mind came a passage from a recent profile on Driver, that had named as perhaps one of his few weaknesses, his tendency to have, 'second-raters' about him. Henry Winterbottom shook his head as if to shake loose the thought and moved from the window to his desk.

He smiled as he recalled how excited Grace had been when he had telephoned her a few minutes ago to tell her of the news that would be released at noon. "Only one more to go," she had said and when he had asked what she had meant, she had chuckled and said, "well, now you are number two, one more and you'll be number one."

He had laughed at his wife, pleased at the faith in him she had always shown, "nonsense m'dear," he had said. "We shall see," she had said confidently. The buzzing of the intercom momentarily startled him, "yes?"

"Sir John Meeling has arrived for his appointment."

"Show him in."

He got up and walked towards the military figure of the Security Chief as he entered the room.

"My dear Sir John, do come in," he said jovially, shaking one of Meeling's hands in both of his. Meeling looked mildly surprised at the warmth of his greeting, but sat down in one of the easy chairs grouped round a long, low, table.

"As it's nearly two weeks now, I thought, as I said to you on the phone, that we should have another chat about the Reid business," Winterbottom said, "I think I told you that the P.M.'s taking a personal interest in this one, and quite frankly, I've not had very much to tell him."

The head of D.I.5 opened the red file on his knee and Winterbottom noticed that it was considerably thicker than the last time he had seen it.

"We haven't been idle," Meeling said crisply, and then said firmly, "I'd prefer to start with the facts."

Winterbottom waved an arm expansively, "as you please."

"It's a financial affair. We are certain about that. It looks as though Mr. Reid fell under the influence of a con-man."

"Good Lord," Winterbottom said, his eyes widening, and his bushy eyebrows shooting up.

"Unfortunately," Meeling went on, "we don't know for certain who he is."

"Won't the Reids tell you?"

"Mr. Reid refuses to say anything and his wife says she knows nothing."

"I find that difficult to believe, knowing Fiona."

"So do I," Meeling said drily, "but there is no way we can force her to say anything."

"Pity," Winterbottom said, and Meeling was not altogether certain whether the Home Secretary found it a pity she would not speak, or a pity that she could not be forced.

"We know that the amount involved is in excess of a quarter of a million pounds and that the Reids are virtually penniless."

The Home Secretary's eyebrows shot up once more. "What about his savings and his house?"

"Gone and mortgaged," Meeling said succinctly.

"How dreadful. I had no idea. We all thought that . . ." His voice tailed off. "How did you discover all this," Winterbottom asked, then became flustered as he saw the look on Meeling's face. "Forget I asked you that question," he said with an embarrassed laugh.

Meeling was not in fact proud of his department's source. It had been given to them on a plate from a contact in the Swiss banking scene who had volunteered the information he had come across, when the news of

Reid's suicide had been publicised. Meeling was hoping that the same source would turn rumour into fact regarding the identity of the con-man.

"You said you weren't certain about the man who fleeced the Reids, do I then take it we are now in the realm of rumour?"

Meeling nodded, wondering how far to go. An unconfirmed whisper had come from the Globe and his men had taken it further. If he was wrong and Phillips was not the man, he would not be very popular in Downing Street and he was only two years away from his pension. If he was right, the information in his possession raised more questions that it answered. He mentally cursed Steve Howland's memory. His assistant had been on Special Branch conference duty eight years ago and when he had seen the photograph of Phillips that Meeling had got from Hong Kong, had identified him as the same man who had briefly been with Richard Driver, who was then a Junior Minister, at that conference. He had particularly remembered him, Howland had said, because it had appeared that Driver was trying to get away from him. A search through the cuttings libraries and several newspapers had finally found a photograph of the delegates in session in which Driver and Phillips could be seen talking together in the corner of the hall.

"Well?" Winterbottom said with a touch of impatience. Meeling made a fast decision. If he was wrong he would have a problem, however, if he was right and the information surfaced publicly from another source he would have an even bigger problem. He also suspected that he would rather enjoy the Home Secretary's reaction. He leant forward in his chair and began to talk.

* * *

Sir Hubert Dugdale looked with frank admiration at Fiona Reid as he helped her to remove her coat. Her phone call first thing that morning had come as a surprise, and he had been intrigued by her sense of urgency together with her promise that he would be greatly interested in what she had to tell him. They had arranged that she would come to Park Lane at 2.15 that afternoon. He had hurried back from a business lunch to be in time for her arrival. She had ignored his invitation to sit down and was wandering around the room, looking at the paintings on the wall and the small pieces of sculpture in the illuminated alcoves. He sensed her nervousness and that, coupled with the tight red dress she was wearing, began to excite him.

"You must have been rather surprised by my call," she said, finally sitting down opposite him. She seemed unaware of her skirt as it rode up her legs as she crossed them, but when he raised his eyes from them and looked at her, she had the faintest of smiles on her face.

"I don't know about surprised, but I was certainly delighted. I've wanted to meet you for a long time."

"Really," she said with a hint of mockery.

"I've met your husband, of course, on several occasions," he went on, "and may I say how distressed I was at what has taken place over the last two weeks. Especially the news of his resignation from the Cabinet which I heard about this lunchtime."

He did not miss, nor was he meant to, the narrowing of the eyes and the tightening of the lips on Fiona Reid's face.

"I imagine," he said encouragingly, "that this is connected with the purpose of your visit?"

"Do you pay for information?" she said suddenly, her face reddening.

"Well now," he said, settling back in his chair, "it depends on the kind of information, and if it's of any value. I presume that you have in mind the Globe as

91

the ultimate recipient?"

She nodded, recrossing her legs.

"How much do you think it is worth?" he said.

"Fifty thousand pounds, paid to me in a Swiss account." she said calmly.

He was jolted and showed it. "That's a great deal of money, Mrs. Reid."

"Please call me Fiona," she said.

"It's a great deal of money no matter what I call you," he said with an attempt at jocularity. "Perhaps you could indicate in some way just what makes you think I may pay so much and, if I may say so, in such an unorthodox manner."

"The information I have if handled properly would most probably mean the resignation of the Prime Minister before the next election." She knew that she had him hooked and she watched as he rose from his chair and started pacing around the room.

"What makes you think I would or could handle it properly?" he said his back towards her as he came to rest in front of the window.

"It's no secret that you are an admirer of Paul Jowett and his party, and I'm sure that you would help him in any way in which you were able. We both know that the only real chance that Jowett would have of winning the next election would be if Driver was no longer Prime Minister."

He turned from the window and gave her a shrewd look, "why are you doing this Fiona?"

She was momentarily flustered. "For fifty thousand pounds. I thought I'd made that clear."

He shook his head slowly, "no, I don't think so. There's more to it than that and for fifty thousand pounds I think I'm entitled to know it all."

"What does it matter what my motives are?" she said her voice rising in anger. "You want the information and I've got it."

92

"You're a very attractive woman," he said, the unexpectedness of the remark catching her by surprise.

"That's the second time I've been told that in twenty-four hours," she said, "but it really has nothing to do with what we are discussing."

He walked over to the easy chair in which she was sitting and stood over her. She had to crane her neck to look up at the tall figure of the newspaper proprietor. A flush slowly suffused her face as she saw the way in which he was gazing down at her, his eyes glittering.

"I'm here to sell information," she said, emphasising the last word. Then as she spread her arms along the back of the easy chair and her breasts strained against her dress, she added, "are you interested?"

He was visibly excited and made an obviously conscious effort to move away from her chair.

"I'd need to know a lot more before I could commit myself to an expenditure of that magnitude, and I should have to be certain that you could satisfy certain conditions." He ran his eyes over her body. "Do you think," he said, "that you could meet all my requirements.?"

She looked him boldly in the eye, and said, "I'm sure I could satisfy you Sir Hubert."

CHAPTER 10

Smiling broadly the Prime Minister walked over to the small crowd gathered at the gates of the northern factory that he had been visiting. Inspector Arthur Wade his detective, was also smiling, but the smile did not reach his eyes which were constantly darting amongst the crowd as he prevented the more enthusiastic members of the public from coming into physical contact with the Prime Minister. It was a good humoured gathering of ordinary people who wanted to see in the flesh, the man they felt they knew so well from the television and newspapers.

Dick Driver was good at meeting the public and he enjoyed it. He exchanged light-hearted banter for a few minutes, ruffling a child's hair and autographing a plaster cast on a young woman's leg.

"We're running an hour late," Andrew Blaine said as the Prime Minister settled next to him in the back of the car.

"Can we trim the list?" the Prime Minister asked him. His private secretary shook his head. "No way. There's a cocktail party in Blackburn followed by the dinner in Preston. You've also promised five minutes to local radio in Blackburn, so the only way we can get back on schedule is by cutting down on the forty-five minutes they gave you to bathe and change."

"Thanks," he said drily, as he lay back in the car and closed his eyes.

It was three days since Fiona Reid had been to see him at Downing Street and he had become increasingly worried as the time had passed. He reviewed yet again what had happened that night and was reasonably satisfied that he had done the right thing. There would have been no end to her demands even if he was capable of fulfilling them. Money he could have found, but the Peerage was a ludicrous request. The image of Fiona leaning towards him in the revealing dress, came into his mind. God, she was a hard bitch. But what could she say. He could always deny knowing Phillips. The bloody man had only been seen with him for a short time at Blackpool all those years ago. Surely he wasn't meant to remember every Tom, Dick or Harry whom he had met in his years in politics? Who would have thought that Phillips would have latched on to Reid. He'd always had an unerring eye for a sucker, and Reid had certainly proved to be a prize one.

She would do something, he was certain of that, and he wished she would make her move. The sooner he rebutted any story she put about the better. He was, he confessed to himself, finding the waiting unnerving.

Perhaps, he comforted himself, it would be best if his very vague connection with Phillips became public and then after his obvious astonishment at the coincidence the whole thing could be laid to rest.

"We're almost there, Sir,"

"Yes," he replied, "we're almost there."

* * *

"Where is he now?" Potts asked.

"On a one day tour up north," Roger Shaw said, through the clenched teeth which were holding his pipe.

"When does he arrive back?"

"Early tomorrow morning, by train. The overnight sleeper."

"Bad organisation isn't it? He'll be back there in a couple of days for conference."

"The word is that he wants to make a strong

impression in the north. This way he appears to be always there."

"Where did you hear that?" Potts asked.

"I just picked it up," Shaw said nonchalantly.

"What else have you just picked up?"

"He's been a bit edgy, the last few days, especially if anyone mentions Reid."

"Really," Potts said, leaning back in his chair and putting his feet on the desk.

He had been nonplussed when Dugdale had told him yesterday that Reid had met Phillips through Driver, and that a close investigation into the connection between Phillips and Driver could be rewarding. Dugdale had been rather smug as well he might, Potts thought ruefully. "I know I'm not a newspaperman or anything like that," he had said, "but I also have my sources, and I'm afraid that at this stage at least, I'm not prepared to reveal them."

He had then gone on to give details of the Conference at which Driver and Phillips were together for a short time, and also revealed that the Prime Minister was attempting to cover up any disclosure of his connection with the dead man. "So," he had concluded, "I suggest that your people start digging."

Potts had only told Shaw of the connection between Driver and Phillips, he had not yet mentioned the cover up.

"I want you to go to Blackpool," he told Shaw.

"For the Conference?"

"Well, I'm not sending you to paddle in the bloody sea."

"What about Ernest Ryecroft?"

"What about him? He's our political editor you're a reporter. In this case one thing has nothing to do with another."

"What do I tell him?" Shaw asked mindful of the secrecy that had been impressed on him by Dugdale and Potts.

"Leave him to me," Potts said, "you just keep an eye on Driver. He's only going for the last two days, but you get there early. See what you can pick up, bearing in mind what we now know."

"Ernest could be a lot of help. He knows far more of that scene that I do."

"No." Potts said firmly. Dugdale had specifically asked him not to tell the political editor, "it's a small world they inhabit and I don't want a chance of even a whisper reaching Driver before we're ready," he had said. Potts suspected that Dugdale was playing a very deep game, but that was his affair. In the meantime he had the chance of being first with a monumental scandal.

"What exactly am I trying to prove?" Shaw asked, whilst half thinking about Anne. Her schedules had been rearranged and she had several days off. He wondered whether she'd come to Blackpool with him.

"You're not trying to prove anything," Potts said. "What you are trying to do is to show that Dick, Mr. 'Wonderful' Driver, may have a few skeletons in the cupboard."

"Don't we all," Shaw said getting up.

Potts studied the handsome fashionably dressed man, "I can imagine the sex of your skeletons," he said, then he hunched his shoulders and reached for a paper from the top of a pile which never seemed to get any smaller.

* * *

Roger Shaw sniffed appreciatively when he opened his flat door that evening. "I've booked a table for half past eight," he called, "thought we'd go out for a good meal."

He ducked as a dishcloth came flying out of the

kitchen. "You're early." Anne said, as he came up behind her and kissed her on the neck as she stood stirring a saucepan which was simmering on the stove. "I was going to have the table laid, candles ready, the whole bit by the time you came home. You haven't really booked a table, have you?" she asked a trifle uncertainly.

He laughed and kissed her again. "Would I do a thing like that after you've told me sixteen times that you were going to show me what a wonderful cook you are?"

She pushed him away. "I'm in no mood for teasing, the sauce won't thicken."

"Will you come to Blackpool with me for a few days?"

"You dirty old man," she said with mock outrage, "anyway what would we do in Blackpool?"

"The same as we do here," he leered, "only the sea air is meant to be bracing."

"You don't need any more bracing," she said dodging out of his way.

Over dinner he told her that he would be working, but that it was a rather vague assignment and they should have plenty of time together. As he was helping her to clear the table she said, "isn't Blackpool near the Lake District?"

"Not a million miles away. Why?"

"Nothing. It's only that I've been all over the world but I've never seen the Lakes. One of the girls on my last trip had just been there for a few days and she was really impressed. Most beautiful part of England she said."

"Perhaps we can steal a day and drive up there," Shaw said, and then with a frown, he stood staring straight ahead, chewing his bottom lip.

"What's the matter Roger?" she said, "have I given you indigestion?"

"No love, the meal was superb." He walked into the bedroom and pulled his notebook from the jacket he had thrown on to the bed and flicked over the pages.

"Bugger me," he said softly to himself as he confirmed what had not before registered but which had obviously been at the back of his mind, released no doubt by Anne's chatter. There is was — Monday August 8th. Not only the day of Phillips's murder, which he had noted a couple of weeks ago, but also one of the dates of the Prime Minister's big sleep. He had only written it down yesterday. After Potts had first told him to start sniffing around the Prime Minister. It was the only unusual thing to have happened to the Prime Minister for some time, as far as Shaw could discover.

He grinned at himself in the mirror on the front of the wardrobe door, "you wanted skeletons, Potty," he said, "how about this one?"

"You're a looney, you know that don't you?" Anne said from the doorway. "Not only do you talk to yourself, but you look into the mirror while you do it."

He lunged towards her and grabbing one of her arms, yanked her squealing on to the bed.

Half an hour later as he lay, stroking her blonde hair, he asked her, "could someone go to Hong Kong and back in two days?"

"They could," she murmured sleepily, "but they would be very tired when they came back. Why?"

"Nothing," he said, "I was just thinking." He was thinking of the other piece of gossip he'd picked up yesterday about the Prime Minister's sleep. Everyone close to him had been surprised at how tired and even haggard, he had looked on his return from the Lakes, considering he had been sleeping for two days.

"No," he muttered, "I am being bloody stupid, must be the wine."

"Looney," she murmured.

"Very probably," he agreed. But he remained wide awake while she slept.

CHAPTER 11

Sir John Meeling strode up Whitehall and turned into Downing Street. There was only a handful of tourists behind the crash barriers opposite the famous front door. They were gazing at the curtained windows and speculating as to the identity of anyone who stopped outside No. 10.

He did not have to ring the bell, and he knew that one of the minor mysteries that intrigued the sightseers was how the door opened when someone approached. He knew, however, that just inside the front door were two rooms, one of which was used by doormen, who saw who was approaching through the window.

He walked through the front door, passing the Chippendale hooded chair in the entrance hall, and started down the long red-carpeted corridor that led to the Cabinet Room. He passed the Grandfather clock by Benson of Whitehaven, the bust of Benjamin Disraeli and the Gainsborough and Van der Velde paintings on the wall.

A secretary appeared and showed him into the anteroom of the Cabinet Room, saying that the P.M. would be free very soon, as the meeting he was chairing was just finishing and apologising for the delay.

The Security Chief thanked him, and walked over to the bust of Wellington. He wondered what the Iron Duke would have done in his position.

When he had received positive confirmation that Phillips had been the con-man involved with Reid, he had spoken to the Home Secretary suggesting that it was necessary to discuss this with the Prime Minister, if for no other reason than that he may be able to shed some further light on the affair.

He had not spelt out to the Home Secretary the difficult position he felt himself to be in, but the Home Secretary had surprised him with his perception. "You are almost in, what I think our American friends would call, a 'no-win' situation," he had said. "I would also feel happier," he had continued, "from a personal point of view, if this were brought out into the open. So I'm afraid you're elected. After all," he had concluded, "if he were not Prime Minister it would just be a routine enquiry."

But he was Prime Minister, he mused, and that was why he was waiting to enter the Cabinet Room at Number 10 Downing Street.

He heard the sound of voices and a moment later the door opened and Andrew Blaine, the Prime Minister's secretary asked him to come in. Sir John had been in the Cabinet Room on several occasions, when he had been called in to advise or to report to the Cabinet on security. But it still rather overwhelmed him.

The Prime Minister was sitting in his chair, the only one with arms, half way down the baize-covered table. Boat-shaped so that everyone sitting at it could be seen and heard by everyone else, the table had on it, leather blotters inscribed 'Cabinet Room, 1st Lord' in front of each chair. There was also a William III silver box and several silver candlesticks along its length.

Over the fireplace behind the Prime Minister was Van Loo's portrait of Sir Robert Walpole.

"Sorry to have kept you waiting, but this is the only time I could squeeze in today. As it is, I'm rather pushed."

Meeling glanced at Andrew Blaine who was hovering uncertainly. The Prime Minister was quick to interpret the look. "O.K. Andy I'll buzz when I'm ready." Blaine nodded amiably at Meeling and went out through the double doors that led to the secretaries rooms.

"I gather that there's some security problem that the Home Secretary prefers me to deal with," the Prime Minister said, looking at Meeling with interest.

The Security Chief nodded. He had been deliberately vague when asking for this meeting and it seemed to be clear from the Prime Minister's remarks, that he had no idea of its purpose.

"So what's it all about?" the Prime Minister leaned back in his chair.

"I am afraid that it concerns Mr. Reid, Sir."

"Oh yes, what has he been up to now?" the Prime Minister said with a smile, but Meeling was sure from many years experience, that the Prime Minister had tensed.

"It is nothing new Sir, but there do appear to be one or two — er — ramifications to his attempted suicide."

The Prime Minister sat forward, elbows on the table, his hands clasped in front of his face.

"I know that Mr. Winterbottom has kept you informed, however I thought it better to tell you the latest development myself."

"I see."

Meeling noted that the Prime Minister was no longer smiling and that the muscles in his face had become taut. "We now have positive identification of the man who defrauded Mr. Reid. His name was Albert Phillips."

Meeling sat perfectly still, watching the Prime Minister. The silence lengthened until the Prime Minister said, "well?"

"I thought the name might mean something to you Sir." Meeling said in clipped, unemotional tones.

The Prime Minister appeared to be thinking, a puzzled frown on his face. "Albert Phillips," he said slowly shaking his head, "no, it doesn't ring any bells with me, Sir John, should it?"

Meeling was convinced that the Prime Minister was

103

lying. It was the cultivated sixth sense that had taken him to the top of the security service, and he had learned to trust his instinct. But why should he lie? Up to this moment he had felt that the Prime Minister's connection could be rationally explained as mere coincidence, but now he was not at all sure.

"I think you met him at a party conference in Blackpool some years ago, Sir."

"Really Sir John, do you expect me to remember everyone I have ever met, especially at a conference? Anyway why is it so important, whether I had met him or not?"

"He's dead Sir."

"So?" Meeling noticed how white the knuckles were, on the clasped hands of the Prime Minister, who as if interpreting the look, unclasped them, picked up his pen and started doodling on a blue pad. Then with a note of exasperation he said, "Sir John, I wish you would come to the point, what exactly are you trying to tell me?"

Meeling reached into the inside pocket of his jacket and withdrew a photograph. He pushed it across the table. The Prime Minister reached forward, picked it up and Meeling saw the colour drain from his face. The Prime Minister seemed mesmerised by the photograph, as Meeling sat impassively watching him.

There was the slightest of tremors in the Prime Minister's voice when he finally looked up and said, "I presume this is Phillips I am talking to."

"Yes Sir."

The Prime Minister considered the photograph again and then said, his voice firmer and his face returning to its normal colour, "I seem to remember him now, I don't think I ever knew his name, so when you talked about Phillips it meant nothing to me."

"Can you remember what you were talking about?"

The Prime Minister frowned in concentration. "I

don't honestly think I can. I must have been a Junior Minister and he was probably pushing something."

"It would be of great help, Sir, if you could try to be more specific."

"I'm sorry, I wish I could help you, but I must have met thousands of people since that photograph was taken. By the way," he said not looking at Meeling, "where did you get it from?"

"Just a piece of luck, Sir."

"Luck?"

"Luck, that we have a photograph of a man for indentification purposes," Sir John said smoothly.

"Well, I'm sorry I can't be of any help," the Prime Minister said, rising from his chair and walking around the table to Meeling who was by now also standing.

"I felt you should see it," Meeling said indicating the photograph on the table, "as I thought it might be an embarrassment if the press got hold of it."

"Very thoughtful of you Sir John. But I can't really see how an eight year old photograph of me talking to a man who was subsequently murdered abroad, could possibly embarrass me. But I certainly appreciate your action in coming to see me. Here," he said going back to the table and then returning with the photograph, "you had better take this with you."

"That's all right Sir," Meeling said opening the door, "we have plenty of copies." He left the room, leaving the Prime Minister looking at the photograph in his hand.

Sir John Meeling left Downing Street turned into Whitehall and walked back to his office.

For the first time for very many years, his ordered and disciplined mind was in turmoil. A relatively routine enquiry had escalated within fifteen minutes to a potentially explosive situation involving the highest in the land, with him right in the middle.

Two years away from his pension he thought, and

I'm going to have to investigate the Prime Minister. In spite of all his experience and years of training, he had found difficulty in showing no outward emotion, when the Prime Minister had said 'a man subsequently murdered abroad.' He had only told the Prime Minister that Phillips had been murdered. He had not mentioned where or how and curiously the Prime Minister had not asked.

Sir John Meeling squared his shoulders and wondered with unaccustomed apprehension where all this was going to lead him.

* * *

After Meeling had left the Cabinet Room, the Prime Minister went back to his chair and sat down heavily. He had been stunned by the photograph, not even being aware of its existence, and he was less than pleased with his reactions.

He tried to think calmly about what had been said, but he found that his mind was racing.

It had to be that bitch Fiona who had put them on to him, but he was not altogether certain, and where had they got the photograph?

He turned it over in his hands but the back was quite plain. What did it matter where it came from he thought, tearing it into shreds and dropping them through his fingers into the waste basket. There was now a definite connection, but so what? But he had felt himself go pale and he knew that Meeling must have noticed.

He reached out to the button which would summon Andrew Blaine, but he did not press it. He had a terrible premonition that everything was going wrong and that he had lost control.

What would Meeling do now? he asked himself, getting out of his chair and wandering towards the bookcases by the large white double doors. He opened one of the bookcases and idly ran his fingers along the spine of the books, presented by former Prime Ministers. Would Meeling now go to the police with his suspicions?

He supposed that if he did he would speak to the Commissioner of Police at New Scotland Yard. What then? A formal interrogation? A statement? He gently closed the bookcase door and walked back to the table.

Andrew Blaine came into the room in response to the Prime Minister's summons, there was a troubled look on his face.

"If you hadn't buzzed, I was going to interrupt," he said.

"Why? What's happened?"

"The President wants to speak to you in ten minutes."

"The President?" the Prime Minister said uncertainly, his mind still on his interview with Meeling.

"President Sloane," Blaine said looking at him with surprise.

The Prime Minister's attention was now focused on what his Private Secretary was saying and he became alert.

"Is it about my trip?"

"I don't think so. There's rather a crisis air about the urgency with which he wants to talk to you."

The Prime Minister sighed. He did not feel up to another crisis just now.

"All right, I'll take it in here, and you'd better be prepared to revise the list."

Blaine nodded and placed several manilla folders in front of the Prime Minister. "Could you try and get through those as soon as possible? One or two of them are becoming urgent."

The Prime Minister put them on one side and said, "I'll do my best, leave them with me."

The phone rang on the trolley behind the Prime Minister and Blaine went round the table and answered it. He handed the receiver of the white telephone to the Prime Minister saying, "it's President Sloane."

"Hello, Dick, how are you?" the President of the United States boomed.

"Very well, Wesley, and you?"

"I was fine until about an hour ago, when one of our spooks came up with a real nasty piece of information."

The Prime Minister's stomach contracted. Surely . . .

"The Russian manoeuvres on the German frontier are not manoeuvres. They are for real." The relief that flooded the Prime Minister was short lived.

"Is your source reliable?"

"As reliable as those goddamned sources ever are?"

The Prime Minister thought swiftly about his last briefing from the Foreign Office. He had them five times a week and the last one had only been yesterday. It had mentioned the massing of Russian troops, but it had also stated quite categorically that it was no more than a full scale major manoeuvre. However tension had been growing between Russia, N.A.T.O. and America ever since the election of Sloane who was a hard-line right winger, but there was nothing that he knew of that would justify the President's information.

"We've heard nothing new over here," he said.

"That's why I'm speaking to you Dick. I'll be calling all the N.A.T.O. countries within the next hour, but naturally I wanted to speak to you first."

The Prime Minister noted, as he was meant to, the implied flattery.

"What do you want from us, Wesley?"

"As much information as you can get. Pull out all the stops political as well as military, because if I'm right we're going to have to react at once. So will you get back to me soonest."

"Of course, and Wesley?"

"Yeah?"

"Thanks."

"That's O.K. Dick, but you get back to me, do you hear?"

The line went dead and then to his mounting shame, the Prime Minister realised that he was once again thinking of Sir John Meeling.

CHAPTER 12

Roger Shaw and Anne Baker finished their late lunch and leaving the restaurant walked hand in hand down the winding main street of Bowness until they came to the shore of Lake Windermere.

They stood looking out over the vast expanse of water of England's largest lake, at the small cabin cruisers bobbing at anchor and at the yachts gliding silently before the gentle breeze.

"It is beautiful, Roger. I'm glad we came."

"So am I," he said squeezing her hand. They had left London early in the morning and had driven directly to Bowness. They planned to spend the day and one night in the area and then drive to Blackpool for the Conference the next morning. He had justified the extra day to Potts as necessary 'background'.

They would have arrived in Bowness much earlier had it not been for trouble with his car. The A.A. man at a service station on the M.6 had said that he had only fixed it temporarily and had advised him to get it properly examined as soon as possible. This was in his mind when he said, "let's find a garage who will look after the car and then, if necessary, we can leave it with them until morning."

She agreed and they slowly ambled back up the hill, to the small car park. They got into the car and he tried to start it. Repeatedly he turned the key, but without success.

"We're stuck here forever," he said dramatically.

"Goody," she said snuggling close to him.

Laughing he disengaged himself from her and got out. He saw a garage further up the hill on the other side of the main road and she joined him as he walked towards it.

He explained the situation to a dour man in the

office who shouted for 'Jack'. A few moments later a cheerful freckled-face young man, wiping his hands on a greasy rag appeared and listened sympathetically to Shaw's story.

"I'll come and have a look," he said.

"Don't be long," the dour man said.

They walked back to the car and Jack fiddled under the bonnet for a while and said, "it's had it."

"What's had it?" Shaw asked.

"Look I'll show you."

A few minutes later Shaw was resigned to the fact that he would be without his car for at least another two days.

"We've got to be in Blackpool tomorrow morning," he said.

Jack pointed up the road, "about a mile and a half up there, in Windermere, there's a car rental place."

"What about my car? We're going back to London from Blackpool."

Jack thought for a moment, then said, "look my wife's from Blackpool, and we were thinking of going over one evening this week, my mother-in-law's not well. You hire a car, go to Blackpool and I'll fix yours, and drive it over and bring back the one you rent."

"That's very good of you," Anne said giving him a dazzling smile.

Jack coloured, "that's O.K. You see it will give me a chance to get away early, if I am returning a customer's car. But you'll have to work out the cost with him," he jerked his thumb in the direction of the garage, "and don't let him sting you."

"I won't and thanks," Shaw said as they strolled back to the garage. "By the way, didn't the Prime Minister used to stay somewhere round here?" he asked.

"Yes at Lamtons, in Storrs Park, at Firth's place," Jack said, "but he won't be staying there any more."

"Why not?" Anne asked, not having been deceived

111

by Shaw's apparent casualness.

"Doctor Firth died a few weeks ago. It was only a few minutes after the Prime Minister had left. There was a proper rumpus round here I can tell you."

"Did you ever see Driver when he stayed here?"

"Oh yes, he often wandered about. He liked going into the old bookshop and would sometimes spend an hour rummaging around in there."

"Did you see him the last time he was here?" Shaw asked.

"No. Funny that. Most of us didn't even know he'd been here till he'd gone. Something about him having a long rest."

"Where is the place he used to stay at? I'd love to see it," Anne said, eyes twinkling mischieviously at Shaw. She did not know what he was after, but she was prepared to play her part.

Jack pointed down the hill giving detailed instructions on how to get to Lamtons, and then he said, "I think it's up for sale now."

At the garage Shaw made arrangements to collect his cases from the car later in the day and fixed a price with the dour man for repairing his car and bringing it to Blackpool.

"What was all that about?" Anne said as they started walking towards Windermere.

"All what?" he said innocently.

"You can't fool me Roger Shaw, this is why you agreed so easily to come here. It's something to do with Driver isn't it?"

He looked down at her feigning distaste. "You have a suspicious mind," he said.

"And you're a bad liar."

He grinned and linking arms they walked into the town of Windermere. The car rental office was in a side street off the main road.

"Good afternoon, can I help you?" a tall willowy

brunette asked Shaw huskily, ignoring Anne Baker by his side.

"I'd like to rent a car for two or three days."

"Certainly sir, what type of model would you like?" she leaned over the counter holding a printed card in front of him.

"That one would do fine," he said pointing.

"Just one moment, and I'll check if there's one available," she disappeared through a door behind the counter and he turned to see Anne leaning seductively towards him.

"What type of model would you like?" she mimicked.

"Shut up. She'll be back in a moment."

"If you as much as smile at her, I'll smash you in the face," she said gangster fashion out of the corner of her mouth.

The woman reappeared and told him that there was a car available for immediate rental and asked for his driving licence. He then told her that he would not be returning the car himself and explained about the arrangement he had made with the garage and Jack.

"That's all right as long as there is not going to be a problem over returning the deposit," she breathed, looking him in the eye.

She then told him of the man who had rented a car and instead of returning it had left it to be picked up in the Bowness car park and when they sent him some money owing to him, it had come back 'address unknown'. Then she had got into trouble from her boss for not checking the return address when he had phoned in, in case they had got it wrong and he was still waiting for his money.

"Anyway it wouldn't surprise me if he wasn't a crook who had used the car for a job," she said as she checked the form that Shaw had filled in.

"What makes you say that?" Shaw said trying not to

smile, conscious of Anne watching him intently.

"Well, when he rented the car he came rushing in just as we were closing and he had a bunch of tissues in front of his face and he was coughing and spluttering all the time he was in here. Honestly," she said looking at Shaw her eyes wide, "I didn't want to go anywhere near him, and then when he bent down to sign the form, I was sure he was wearing a wig."

"You certainly notice things," Anne Baker said coldly.

The woman looked at her for a few moments and said, "you'd be surprised. For instance, I know where he went."

As both Shaw and Anne stayed silent, she went on, "he'd been to Heathrow Airport."

Roger Shaw suddenly stiffened. "How could you know that?"

"Easy," she said triumphantly, "I hired a car from here in July to go to Heathrow when I went on holiday and I remember that his mileage was exactly the same as mine. You see," she said lowering her voice, "I left working out my account for a month as I'd overspent on holiday and didn't want to have to pay so it just happened that I calculated both accounts on the same day."

"When was this?" Shaw asked casually.

"First week in August. Our busiest week."

As she turned to select a key from a board on the wall, Shaw gave Anne a warning look and she recognised that he was serious.

"Who was he, this crook of yours?" he said smiling at the woman.

"Oh he said he came from London," she said, warming to his charm.

"Really? Whereabouts? We're from London."

"Ealing I think."

"What a coincidence, that's where my brother

lives."

"Just a second, I've got it here," she opened a box file and rifled through the papers. "Here we are, Brian Hutchinson, 39 Bix Road, Ealing."

"Bix Road? No I don't know that one."

"Anyway," she said looking at him directly, "I'm sure you live in a proper place."

"Very proper," Anne said firmly.

The woman gave her a haughty look and with a 'follow me please' took them outside and handed over the Ford car.

After he had driven a few hundred yards, Shaw pulled up by the roadside, took his notebook from his pocket and made an entry.

"What do you want to write down a false name and address for?" Anne said peering over his shoulder.

He turned to her, his face serious. "Listen Anne, I can't tell you everything but I may be on to the biggest story of my life and I want you to help me."

"Of course I will," she said her eyes shining, "what do you want me to do?"

"Pretend we're married," he said.

"Only pretend," she pouted, and there was a short embarrassed silence.

"We are going to Lamtons," he went on, "and we are considering buying it. So back me up, whatever I say."

"Yes sir," she said as she saluted, trying to restore the previously lighthearted atmosphere.

Ten minutes later he drove into the long drive at Lamtons, and they both got out and looked at the ivy covered house in the spacious grounds.

"I really would like to buy it," she said wistfully as they approached the front door.

The door was opened in response to his ring and the late Dr. Firth's housekeeper looked at the attractive young couple facing her.

"I know this is an awful cheek," Shaw began with his most winning smile, "but my wife and I saw this house this morning and simply fell in love with it. Then over lunch someone said they thought it was for sale, and we were wondering . . ." He looked at her expectantly.

"I'm sorry," she said pleasantly but beginning to close the door, "it is not for sale just yet and when it is, Mr. Deakin at the Agents will be looking after it, you'll have to see him."

"Please," he said quickly as the door was about to close, "we're from London and by the time we hear that it is up for sale it will be gone. Couldn't you let us look round now and then we could deal with the agent over the telephone."

Nell Patterson hesitated, as the couple holding hands looked pleadingly at her.

"All right," she said opening the door, "but you're the first people to see it. I don't know what Mr. Deakin will say, I've told him I don't want anyone round just yet."

"Thank you Mrs. .. . .?" Anne said.

"Miss Patterson. This was Dr. Firth's house and I was his housekeeper. I can stay here until I'm ready to move."

"When do you think that will be?" Anne asked earnestly.

"I've been well provided for, and I'm buying a cottage near Keswick, where my sister lives. I expect to move in the New Year."

They went through the rooms and Anne constantly admired the way in which the house had been looked after and how clean and fresh it was. Shaw was not surprised, after they had all trooped in from the garden, when the housekeeper who had been in animated conversation with Anne, diffidently asked if they would like some tea.

They sat in the kitchen, at Anne's insistence, and

when they all had a cup of tea and a buttered scone in front of them, Shaw asked, "did the Prime Minister ever eat in here?" The housekeeper had mentioned his visits when she had shown them the bedroom he used.

"Sometimes, he'd come in and ask for a soft drink from the fridge and he'd drink it here. But he's a strange man."

"Is he?" Anne said. "I've only seen him on television."

"Oh, he's a fine man, the doctor was very fond of him, but he doesn't like people to see him unless he's neat and tidy. Know what I mean?"

"Not exactly," Shaw said encouragingly.

"Well, like the last time he was here. He was very tired and the Doctor gave him something to make him sleep. And do you know, he slept for over two days."

"Two days," Anne said in astonishment.

"Well he was in his room for two days and the doctor said he was sleeping. But that's what I mean. He had a large bowl of fruit and I think the doctor took him in two or three drinks, but he didn't want anyone else to see him half-asleep and unshaved. I suppose he didn't mind the doctor because he was a doctor."

"How strange," Shaw said.

"Yes it was, and I don't mind telling you I was a bit hurt."

Anne put her hand on the older woman's arm, "you shouldn't be upset Miss Patterson, I'm sure he didn't mean anything personal."

"Then he gave everyone a shock by just walking in from the garden like that."

"From the garden?"

"Yes. One minute he's in his room asleep, the next he's coming through the french window, looking as if he could do with a night's sleep, never mind having been asleep for two days. Nobody heard him get up or go out and Arthur was very surprised."

"Arthur?"

"Inspector Wade, he's the Prime Minister's body-guard."

She suddenly seemed to realise that she had been talking too much and Shaw, who was about to press her further, decided not to ask any more questions. He imagined that she was lonely in the house on her own and had unburdened herself to them due mainly to Anne's sympathetic understanding. They talked about the house and the Lakes and then Nell Patterson walked them to their car.

"I hope you buy it," she said through the open car window, "I'm sure you would both be very happy here."

"I'm sure we would," Anne said, then turning to Shaw asked, "don't you think so darling?"

"I do," he said, "in fact in the short time we've been here, I've felt very happy. Very happy indeed."

CHAPTER 13

"I know several of you want to get to Blackpool tonight, but this could blow up into a full scale international crisis."

The Prime Minister looked at the members of his Cabinet sitting in their places round the baize boat-shaped table in the Cabinet Room.

"President Sloan," he went on, "is most concerned and is advocating an immediate reaction." He raised his hand to silence the sudden babble of protest, "I have informed him, that we would be loath to go along with him on the information we have."

"He's in trouble at home," the Foreign Secretary drawled, "and a major scare would take the heat off him for a while. I suggest we are not stampeded by him into doing something foolish."

"That's all very well," Humphrey Maxton the Chancellor of the Exchequer said in his precise tones, "but what if he is correct?"

The Prime Minister let the discussion run on ensuring that everyone had an opportunity of making his point. He privately agreed with Douglas Burn, the Foreign Secretary, in thinking that the President was not above turning the Russian manoeuvre into a crisis, if it would help him at home. The President was asking, even demanding, that all N.A.T.O. troops went on to a final stage alert. The Prime Minister knew that this would escalate the situation to such an extent, that if there was no genuine crisis now, there would be then. The trouble was, he thought, that Wesley Sloane and Vladimir Provitch, the Russian leader, hated each other. An early summit meeting between the two, shortly after Sloane had been elected which had only been a few weeks after Provitch had come to power, had gone disastrously wrong, with charges and counter accusations of bad faith, broken understandings and general ill will being bandied about for several weeks after it had finished.

The Prime Minister remembered the acid way in which Sloane had described Provitch to him in confidence as a boorish, ignorant and charmless peasant. He had therefore been very surprised when on his own first meeting with the Russian leader he had found a cultivated, educated but hard man, far different from the old revolutionaries who had preceded him, both in temperament and outlook. But it did not take Provitch long to make his feelings about Sloane crystal clear. At the time he had found it all mildly amusing but now it was no longer funny. He doubted whether either of them would rush to speak to each other on the 'hot line', without a great deal of pressure being brought to bear on them.

He rubbed his eyes and then stretched clasping his hands behind his neck. He caught sight of the Home Secretary looking at him out of the corner of his eye and recalled that Winterbottom had been looking at him rather strangely throughout the Cabinet meeting. He wondered how much Meeling had told Winterbottom, but then he tried ruthlessly to banish the thought. He was aware of a silence and he found that they were all looking at him.

"I'm sorry," he said, "I was thinking about something else for a moment."

"I suggested," the Foreign Secretary said, "that it might be an idea if you spoke to Provitch. You would probably get more out of him than Sloane."

The Prime Minister paid close attention for the rest of the discussion and then crisply and decisively summed up the general feeling of the members of the Cabinet. He brought the meeting to a close, telling them to stay in close touch so that he could keep them informed of any progress he might make or of any further developments in the situation.

As they were leaving he motioned to the Home Secretary to remain behind.

"I won't keep you a moment Henry," he said when they were alone, "but I want a word about the wretched Reid business," He noticed the Home Secretary's discomfiture but did not comment on it. "Sir John Meeling came to see me this morning as you probably know," he waited a moment but Winterbottom stayed silent, "I would appreciate your views."

"It's sad — er — very sad — er — the whole business," Winterbottom said, not looking at the Prime Minister.

"I agree. By the way Henry, did you know that apparently I met this rogue Phillips years ago? Didn't remember him of course, just another hanger-on."

Relief flooded the Home Secretary's face, and the Prime Minister was aware of the strain he must have been under, not knowing how much he was supposed to have been told.

"Anyway I think it's time to close the book."

The Home Secretary looked uncertainly at the Prime Minister. "Close the book?"

"Yes. There's no point in raking over dead ashes. Poor old Peter Reid is finished and Phillips is dead but should the press get hold of the fact that I knew him, well . . ." he spread his hands expressively.

"But what about Reid?"

"What about him? It's nothing to do with us. I mean, we don't need the head of D.I.5 investigating the affairs of a dead con man. If Peter Reid wants to press charges, I suppose the police would look into it, but as far as I know he has no intention of doing so."

"The Home Secretary was looking unhappy. "I got the impression that Sir John would like to tie up a few loose ends."

"And I'm telling you to forget it. As I say close the book. If it becomes known that Meeling is investigating Reid the rumours will start to fly and we don't need them — especially with a possible Russian crisis on our hands and an imminent party conference."

"I do see that, of course, but . . ."

"But nothing, Henry, tell Meeling to drop it. Otherwise he's likely to do us more harm than good."

"Very well, Prime Minister, if that's what you want."

"Yes it is. Now then Henry when I'm in Washington and you are in charge . . ."

The Prime Minister watched the Home Secretary leave the Cabinet Room a happier man after having had his ego massaged for ten minutes.

He also felt a great deal happier now that he had closed the Reid file and stopped Meeling from making any further enquiries. With a bit of luck that would be the last he would hear of Phillips and all the petty problems that went with him. Now he could concentrate on the real problems — problems that perhaps only he could solve for a grateful country and an admiring world.

* * *

Sir John Meeling replaced the receiver on the telephone and switched off the recording machine. He glanced at his watch, looked out of the window and decided to go for a walk in St. James' Park.

It was becoming more complicated than even he had feared. The call he had just received from the Home Secretary telling him to drop the Reid and Phillips enquiry had not altogether surprised him. He had anticipated that Driver would try to stop him, but had not thought that he would use Winterbottom. He must be feeling very confident, Meeling thought, to be as blatant as that. He was curious as to what Winterbottom had really thought. He had sounded almost apologetic on the phone, but he had been quite adamant. He wondered how Driver had primed him, but then he smiled wryly to himself as he recognised the enormous power of patronage that was in the hands of the Prime Minister.

He walked slowly through the park trying to determine his next move.

He had, as he saw it, several options open to him. He could abide by the instructions given to him by Winterbottom. He could ignore them and pursue his investigation on a semi-official basis. He could pass on his suspicions to the Commissioner of Police. Or he could officially close the file and carry on totally unofficially, with all the attendant risks that that would entail.

He turned his face to the warm September sun as he walked. He dismissed the idea of closing the file with hardly a moment's thought. To carry on within the department after having been officially told to stop, could endanger other careers as well as his own. As far as the police were concerned, he had no more than conjectures to give them and he doubted if they would be in any great hurry to grasp such a nettle as the one he would be offering.

That only seemed to leave one course open to him, he thought as he turned about and started walking back the way he had come. But what had he really got to justify the risk he would be taking by continuing the investigation privately?

Only a strong conviction that the Prime Minister had known Phillips far better than he had admitted, that he had deliberately lied in defence of his claim and that he had subsequently attempted to squash any further investigation into the affair.

So why was he bothered? Meeling asked himself. With only two years to his pension what was he trying to prove, and to whom?

If he started this sort of hare he would be very much alone, with no one to turn to for advice or help. But, he thought to himself with quiet satisfaction, he had never been party to a cover-up in the whole of his career. There had been the necessary bending of the rules from time to time and even the occasional dropping of cases in return for help received in other matters. These were the nuts and bolts of day to day security, but now he felt that he was being asked to deliberately suppress something purely to keep a politician in power.

By the time he had returned to his office Sir John Meeling knew what he was going to do and why he was going to do it.

* * *

"Why did he do it?" Douglas Burn, the Foreign Secretary asked the Prime Minister, his drawl noticeably less pronounced, as they sat facing each other in the first floor study at Number 10 Downing Street.

"Who knows? He's got his pressures just as we have." The Prime Minister had been staggered and then angry when he had heard that President Sloane had placed all American troops on full scale alert without any further international consultation.

Within the hour the Soviet Union announced that it had officially cancelled the huge Eastern European manoeuvres and that its troops were instead, 'now in an active state of readiness'. He had tried to speak to Sloane but the American President was 'unavailable at this time'. Most of the European leaders had spoken to each other in the past hour, but the suddenness of the crisis had caught them unawares and there was confusion amongst them as to how they should respond.

"I think you should contact Provitch," the Foreign

Secretary said. "I know I suggested it at Cabinet and there was a lukewarm reaction to the idea but now I think it's more important than ever. I've discussed it with my people and they are all for it."

"Suggest what?" the Prime Minister said.

"I'm not sure you could suggest anything, but you may be able to create an atmosphere where at least Sloane and Provitch would talk to each other. It wouldn't surprise me," the Foreign Secretary continued, "if Sloane isn't scared stiff at what has happened. He's new, and probably the temptation to flex his international muscles proved too much for him, especially if he thought it might help him domestically."

"And Provitch?"

"Difficult. The trouble is that he is also new and we don't yet know all that much about him. However from all the information we have, it appears very doubtful whether he wants any real trouble just now. But of course, it's just because he is new that he must respond to any challenge and not appear to be weak."

The Prime Minister was thoughtful for a few moments and then said, "supposing I was to get an immediate invitation to Moscow, how would that affect Conference?"

The Foreign Secretary looked startled. "How are you going to do that?" then considering the implications he went on, "if you could try to put in an appearance at Blackpool I can't see that anyone could criticise you for missing Conference, and it will certainly help me in the foreign affairs debate."

"Right," the Prime Minister said decisively, reaching for the telephone, "let's see if we can set up a call to Provitch."

CHAPTER 14

Roger Shaw cursed softly to himself as he replaced the receiver of the bedside telephone. He walked over to the window and looked out at the sea crashing on to the deserted beach under a leaden sky.

Due to the party conference all the hotels at Blackpool had been fully booked and he had considered himself lucky in getting a room in a hotel in St. Annes a few miles down the coast.

He turned as he heard a key scraping in the lock.

"Phew, it's like the Arctic out there," Anne said dumping a pile of parcels on the bed. She kicked off her shoes as she came over and kissed him.

"I didn't expect to find you here just yet," she said.

"I didn't expect to be here, but as glamour boy has gone to Moscow, there was nothing much for me to do in Blackpool. So I thought I'd come back here and do some useful telephoning."

"And was it?"

"Was it what?"

"Useful."

"No, it decidedly wasn't."

She kissed him again, "calm down and tell Auntie Anne about it."

"Some Auntie."

"That's better," she said pleased at having made him smile, "now what was making you look so fierce?"

"British Airways amongst other things," he said. Then clasping his hand to his forehead, he looked at her and said, "now why on earth didn't I think of you before."

"There's no answer to that," she said.

"Listen, Auntie, do you know anyone who has

access to airline computers?"

"I may," she said guardedly, "it depends what you want."

"I want to check the passenger lists on all flights to Hong Kong that left Heathrow on Sunday 7th August and those that came back on Monday 8th August."

"How do you mean, check?" she asked.

"Check a name."

She thought for a moment and then said, "have you tried?"

"Yes, I have. They told me they would only give out that kind of information to the police. I tried everything, but they wouldn't budge."

She looked at her watch, "it's getting a bit late but I can try."

She dialled directory enquiries gave a department of British Airways and asked for its telephone number. She then dialled again and asked for Deidre Lomax.

"Hello Deidre, this is Anne. — Fine thanks — Blackpool — yes I did say Blackpool. No, you don't know him," she coloured slightly as Shaw raised his eyebrows at her. "Look, Deidre, can you do me a favour? I want to know if . . ." she paused as Shaw quickly wrote in his notebook and gave it to her, "if a Brian Hutchinson went to Hong Kong from Heathrow on August 7th and came back August 8th." She hesitated for a short time and then said, "yes, I know, but it is important to this friend of mine and therefore," she added softly, "important to me."

"What about other airlines," Shaw mouthed at her.

"Deidre, one other thing, could you check with any other carrier who operated on those dates?"

She suddenly held the receiver away from her ear and Shaw could hear the squawking coming from it.

"Deidre! Where did you learn words like that?"

She laughed at something that was said in return and after a few further pleasantries, she gave the hotel telephone number and hung up.

"Who is Deidre?" he asked solemnly, "and why has she never heard of me?"

"I keep very quiet about you," she said darkly, "especially to Deidre Lomax. She used to be a stewardess and we became close friends even though she always seemed to like my friends better than hers, but then she got fed-up with the hours and got herself transferred to administation. She knows everybody and if anyone can find out about . . ." she glanced at the notebook she was still holding ". . .Brian Hutchinson. she can. Now then, who is he, this mysterious passenger? Isn't this the name that you wangled out of Varda the Vamp at the car rental place?"

"Correct. But let's leave it, for the moment. I may be on the wrong tack. Now then what do you want to do this evening?.."

* * *

It was nearly midnight when they returned to their hotel after a long and expensive dinner at a well known restaurant in the town.

As he collected the room key, the clerk gave a telephone message to Anne. She read it, frowned and gave it to Shaw. He felt the pleasure and contentedness he had been feeling during dinner leave him as he read, 'checked all carriers, and no record of your man. Deidre.'

He lay awake, worrying at the problem. He felt sure he was right but somehow he had missed something.

He knew that Anne was also awake though silent and he felt a moment's guilt at the perfunctory way in which he had earlier made love to her.

"Do you want to talk?" she whispered.

128

"Yes," he whispered back. They both laughed and then she said in a normal voice, "perhaps he went by private plane."

"To Hong Kong?" he said incredulously.

"No I suppose not. But wait a minute," she sat up excitedly, "he may not have gone direct."

"How do you mean?"

"Supposing he went via somewhere else, Paris, Rome, Delhi, Bangkok. Deidre only checked on direct flights."

He too was now sitting up having caught some of her excitement.

"But it would be impossible to check every connection."

"Not if we worked backwards. If you know the day he arrived, we can check the carriers flying into Hong Kong on that day. Once we've done that, we know where he boarded and therefore know the route he took. I'll get on to Deidre first thing in the morning."

"It's asking a lot."

"She'll do it," Anne said with determination, "or else."

"Or else what?" he said, chuckling at her manner.

"Never you mind."

This time their lovemaking was far more satisfactory.

* * *

Sir Hubert Dugdale howled with pain and shock as he felt the blood running from the deep scratch on his face.

He backed away as a furious Fiona Reid advanced on him, naked apart from her shoes..

"What the hell do you think you're doing?" she raged rubbing the livid weal on her shoulder. "If you as much as lay another finger on me, I'll kill you. Do you understand?" she screamed, "I'll kill you."

She thrust him out of his bedroom at the Park Lane flat, and he heard her lock the door.

He stood helplessly for a moment in his underwear and tried to gather his wits. Then pouring a large brandy he drained the glass in a succession of quick nervous gulps. This was to have been the night when Fiona Reid delivered the unspoken part of their bargain, he thought miserably as he looked at the closed and locked door.

He had become progressively more excited as the evening had worn on and he had been waiting for the moment when in his own way he would tame the haughty woman with whom he had been dealing over the last few days.

He had enjoyed his negotiations with her, protracting them unnecessarily, as he had from the first, made up his mind to come to an arrangement with her.

The idea of having the wife of the former Deputy Prime Minister at his mercy, had been too much for him to resist, and the information that she had, though not conclusive in itself, was sufficient to prove that the Prime Minister was involved in some sort of cover-up.

But primarily it had been Fiona Reid herself that he had wanted. He had thought he had made it clear, by oblique hints and turns of phrase, the type of sex he favoured and he had been totally unprepared for her reaction when he had first hit her.

She unlocked the door and came out of the bedroom fully dressed.

"You're — not — going?" he stammered weakly, a note of entreaty in his voice.

She looked at him pityingly. "You're sick, but that's your problem. I don't have to be part of your illness. I'm going now, and I don't think we ever need to see or speak to each other again."

"What about our bargain?" he said, quickly

recovering his normal manner.

"What about it?" she said moving towards the door, "there was no mention of any violence as far as I can recall, and anyway you don't seem to have kept to your side."

"In what way?"

She stood holding the door handle. "In addition to the money which I already have," she said with a hint of satisfaction, "you were also going to expose Driver for what he is. But I've seen nothing in the paper. On the contrary it's full of praise and adulation about how he is going to save the world." Her voice rose and there was a vicious edge to it when she said, "you promised to destroy him, but he's getting bigger." Then she shrugged and looking at him contemptuously as he stood in his underclothing she said, "I obviously made a mistake, you're only capable of hitting women." She opened the door and slammed it closed behind her.

He stood looking at the door then his anger swelled in his head, ran down his throat and curled into a small tight ball in his chest. His hands began to tremble, as he realised that she had cheated him. He walked into the bedroom and looking in the mirror he saw the long, deep gash on the side of his face. His anger slowly subsided to be replaced with an ice cold hate, that seemed to pervade the whole of his body. He should have known that they were all the same. Reid, Driver, all of a type. The whole party thought that they were born to rule. How dare she look at him like that, as if he was dirt. She had been quite prepared to take his money but now she thought she could walk away. She wanted Driver destroyed did she? The trace of a smile hovered around his lips as an idea slowly began to form, but then the sense of outrage at what she had done once more took possession of him.

After he had bathed his face and put on a plaster dressing he picked up the blue telephone on his desk and dialled a number.

"Maxine? You know who this is? What do you mean you're tired? I want you to come now. What? Oh I see," he said slowly, his hands beginning to tremble as he recognised the possibility of a second rejection.

"Now listen Maxine. I'll pay you double and . . ." his voice overrode her as she tried to interrupt, "a large bonus." He listened for a moment and then nodded to himself in satisfaction as he heard her reluctant agreement.

* * *

"God Almighty," the young house doctor muttered as he gently cut away the clothes from the unconscious young woman who had been brought in by ambulance, after having collapsed in Park Lane.

"Who is she?" he asked the nurse who was assisting him.

"There were a couple of letters addressed to Maxine Lambert, in her handbag," the nurse said tight-lipped as finally all the clothes were removed and the full horror of the woman's injuries were revealed.

"Professional?"

"She was carrying a large amount of money."

"She'll be lucky if she lives to spend it." he said sadly shaking his head.

CHAPTER 15

The conference chairman was handed a piece of paper and immediately interrupted the speaker at the rostrum below him.

"I am sorry to break in, but I thought delegates should know that the Prime Minister is in the building" he said as he looked expectantly to the side of the stage. There was an immediate hubbub as the thousands of seated delegates looked in the same direction as they noisily rose to their feet.

Photographers jostled for position in the gangways below the rostrum, and the television cameras throughout the hall swung so that their lenses were pointing in the direction towards which everyone was looking.

The excitement in the vast hall mounted as the delegates, journalists, observers, and technicians craned their heads to catch the first glimpse of the man who had in the last two days captured not only most of the headlines, in newspapers around the world, but also the imagination of most of their readers.

They were waiting to see the man described within the last forty-eight hours by Vladimir Provitch, the Soviet leader, as 'perhaps the only man who could have achieved this extraordinary breakthrough'. One hour later President Wesley Sloane had said, 'the first point on which I entirely agree with Vladimir Provitch, and let us hope it is the first of many, is in his description of the British Prime Minister.' The noise gradually swelled as movement was detected at the side of the stage. Moments later the Prime Minister appeared flanked by the Party chairman and the Home Secretary, in his capacity as Deputy Prime Minister.

The boyish face was wreathed in smiles, although the more sharp-eyed among the stamping, cheering crowd had already observed how tired he looked. He made his way slowly along the front row of the platform, shaking hands and clasping shoulders, until he came to the place that had been made ready for him.

He stood looking out over the sea of upturned faces as the ovation went on, and not for the first time reflected how lucky he was.

On his arrival at Moscow, he knew that he was going to be used by the Russians as an instrument by which they would achieve their object and he went along happily with them.

He had been met at the airport by Provitch and his welcome had almost been that of a Head of State and he had immediately appreciated that the Russians would have to build him up in order to justify their co-operation with his peace-keeping mission.

When he, Provitch and the interpreter had finally been alone in the Kremlin, they had sat looking at each other across the wide expanse of table. Then Provitch had launched into a tirade of ridicule and abuse against the American President which had however, lacked real intensity.

At first Provitch had refused to even consider a dialogue with Sloane but Driver had carried on feeling as though he were an actor in a play, where the words had to be said for the play to be performed. Then towards the end of a long dinner Provitch had indicated that if Sloane stood down his troops the Soviets would in their turn revert to their manoeuvre and disperse.

He had spoken to the President within the hour, who had refused to negotiate over the phone and had virtually demanded that the Prime Minister fly directly to Washington so that there could be an assessment 'on a one-to-one basis of what that lunatic Provitch is offering'.

He had left at dawn for the American capital together with the handful of aides who had accompanied him to Moscow. Don Parrish his Press Secretary, was among his party and had already managed to launch the 'international statesman' image that was already being picked up by the world's press, encouraged by the helpful Russians, who felt that it suited their purpose.

Their arrival in Washington had been as impressive as the one they had received in Moscow, with the President waiting to receive the Prime Minister as he helicoptered on to the White House lawn to the sound of a military band and a nineteen gun salute.

There was no doubt that the President wanted everything back to normal and that he regretted what had been described as his 'adventure'. Behind the bluster and tough talk, the Prime Minister had recognised the same desire as he had observed in Provitch to undo what had been done.

Sloane had listened carefully to his report of his meeting with Provitch and after four hours of talks agreed to the proposals providing a suitable time-table could be worked out.

As he stood occasionally waving, the ovation showed no signs of abating and he once more reflected that he had been the right man in the right place at the right time. But deep down in his mind he half wondered if there were not more to it than that. Surely he must have had some ability, some spark of — of greatness which made the American and Russian leaders feel that they could trust him.

He turned to wave to the people lining the side wall of the hall when he caught sight of one man who was not clapping or cheering. He faltered in mid-wave and he felt his smile slip as he fleetingly wondered what Sir John Meeling was doing at the Party Conference in

Blackpool.

* * *

The Security Chief had noticed the momentary hesitation when the Prime Minister had recognised him during the ovation, later to be described as the longest and most fervent any leader had received at any Party Conference. While it was still continuing he slipped quietly from the hall and made his way out of the building and walked down the road until he came to the wide promenade. It was a blustery day and his silver hair became quickly windswept as he walked. He had come to Blackpool on what he had admitted to himself as being a rather lame excuse, that of checking the security arrangements of the senior members of the government who were attending their Party Conference. It had not deceived his assistant Steve Howland who had made several attempts to find out what was in his mind and had showed mild annoyance at his chief's unaccustomed reticence.

It had not been a wasted trip, he thought as he walked, leaning slightly into the strong wind.

He had only spoken to Inspector Arthur Wade, the Prime Minister's personal detective for a few minutes, but it had been long enough to extract from the Inspector what he had wanted to know.

"Are you satisfied from your experience, with the overall arrangements for the security of the Prime Minister?" he had asked him. The Inspector slightly surprised at the question had thought for a while and offered a few suggestions. Then Meeling had said, "what about the times when the Prime Minister is on holiday? For instance you spent a few days in this part of the world not so long ago didn't you?"

The Inspector had laughed, "I wish all the P.M.'s

holidays were as restful as that one. I never saw him for two days," and then seeing the raised eyebrows had quickly added, "oh I knew where he was Sir, all the time. He was in bed sleeping, and the late Dr. Firth looked after him."

"Didn't you see him at all during those two days?"

"No Sir. Should I have done?" the Inspector had asked obviously puzzled by the question. Meeling had quickly diverted the conversation away from the topic, and with a few words of encouragement he had left the Inspector and gone into the hall in time to see the triumphant entry of the Prime Minister.

Now he turned about and with the wind in his back he briskly walked to where he had parked his car.

It took him just over an hour to drive to the Belsfield Hotel in Bowness. He parked in the hotel car park and went into the hotel. He booked himself a table for dinner later that evening and asked the way to Storrs Park.

He followed the directions he had been given and a ten minute walk brought him to Lamtons. He consulted a small notebook which he took from his pocket and then he walked down the drive until he came to the front door. He rang the bell and waited. He rang again and also knocked with the large brass knocker, but still no one came to the door.

He walked round to the side of the house and noticed that all the windows were closed. He strolled down the lawn until he came to the water's edge. He wandered over to the Boat House and looked through the window, then he walked back the way he had come, rang the bell once more and then when there was still no answer he walked back up the drive to the road.

He had walked a few yards down the road when he noticed a small gate. He opened it and found himself on a small track between the Lamtons hedge and the wall of the house next door. He picked his way down it until he came to the side wall of the building, in which there was a small window. He looked through and realised he was on the other side of Lamtons Boat House.

There was a thoughtful look on his face as he made his way back to the road. He had not walked far when a small car passed him and he heard it slow down, he looked back in time to see it turn into the driveway at Lamtons.

He carried on walking slowly away from Lamtons and a minute or two later the little car passed him. He turned back and walking swiftly was soon once more ringing the bell. The door was opened by a woman who was wearing an outdoor coat.

"Miss Patterson," he said politely, having noted her name from the security survey done prior to the Prime Minister's visit.

"Yes?" she said enquiringly.

"I wonder if I may have a few words with you? I'm sorry to arrive like this, but I did try to telephone but there was no reply," he lied.

"No, there wouldn't be, my nephew has only just brought me back."

"May I come in?"

She looked at him uncertainly, and he said, "please forgive me, I should have shown you this straight away." He brought a document from his pocket and gave it to her.

She read it slowly gave it back to him and opened the door wide. "I shouldn't have thought that security would be interested in this place anymore," she said as she led him into the sitting room. "Now that Dr. Firth is dead, I don't suppose the Prime Minister will ever stay here again."

"It's not the future in which we're interested, it's more the immediate past," he said with an enigmatic smile.

"What do you mean?"

He considered her carefully for a few moments and then said, "I'm sure I don't have to tell you how confidential this conversation must be."

"I know how to hold my tongue," she said tartly.

"Oh we know that, Miss Patterson, "that's why I'm prepared to confide in you," he said disarmingly.

She nodded, partly mollified and waited for him to continue.

"When the Prime Minister returned to London from here, it was discovered that some highly confidential papers were missing. It was thought up to now, that they had been mislaid in London, but we are now beginning to wonder if they had been lost here."

"If I'd come across anything that had been left behind I would have let someone know immediately, but I've found nothing."

He appeared to be very disappointed and she went on helpfully, "have you tried the Belsfield, all the secretaries and such like stayed there?"

"Not yet, I'm having dinner there this evening, and I'll make some enquiries then. I was hoping that you would have been able to help me."

"I'm sorry," she said, "and in any case the Prime Minister hardly did any work at all on his last visit, so there wouldn't be many papers in the house."

"Yes I know," he said, "I understand he was sleeping most of the time."

"That's right. He didn't even need any of your security, but Arthur — I mean Inspector Wade didn't mind, he also had a good rest."

He had picked up a note in her voice when she had referred to Wade.

"Arthur is a good man," he said firmly.

"Do you know him?" she said with more animation

than she had previously shown.

"Of course, he's one of our best men, that's why he's so upset about the missing papers," he improvised.

"What have they got to do with him?" she asked with a frown.

"Nothing directly, but he was the security man on the spot, so to speak." He let the silence lengthen and then said, "ah well, I'll have to see what I can find out at the hotel."

He was genuinely disappointed. He did not know why, but he had hoped that by seeing Lamtons and talking to the housekeeper, he would have moved forward. He was a great believer in absorbing the atmosphere of places and in meeting the people involved in his work and it had hitherto proved rewarding.

As they were walking across the hall towards the front door he said, "are you going to continue living here alone?"

She told him about the cottage in Keswick and living near her sister, and that she was now starting to clear up the house prior to its being sold.

"Everything is going to be sold, house and contents, and whatever the buyer of the house doesn't want is going to be auctioned."

"You've got quite a job on your hands," he said looking round.

"Yes, it's surprising the junk that accumulates over the years in a house like this."

She opened the front door and walked outside with him, "I've already made a start, by clearing out the Boat House," she hesitated for a moment, then said, "there is one thing, I know it's nothing to do with you, but for the life of me I don't know where it came from."

"What is it?"

"An almost new case, with a suit, one or two other things, and, believe it or not, a wig."

He stopped walking and casually said, "where was it?"

"Under a dirty old tarpaulin in the Boat House, I can't imagine who put it there or why."

"Where is it now?"

"In the box room, do you want to see it?"

"Well if you think I can be of any help," he said turning and walking back with her into the house, "you never know, I may have one or two ideas."

CHAPTER 16

Philip Melrose Vivian Potts reached over to the intercom pressed a button and said, "I don't want to be disturbed under any circumstances." He then got up from behind his desk and opened a window.

Roger Shaw had noted with amusement that his editor had not complained this time when he had brought out his pipe, and lit it. Potts walked back from the window and leaned on his desk in front of Shaw.

"Who else have you told?"

"No one," Shaw replied sharply.

"All right, don't get heated. What about your girl friend?"

"I've not discussed it with her, but she's no fool and it is possible she may suspect something."

"Can you trust her?"

Shaw found himself smiling, "oh yes, she can be trusted."

Potts grunted, then said, "now let's see what we have actually got," He went behind his desk, and sat down in the large swivel chair.

"One. We know it's possible to go from Bowness to Hong Kong and back in a little over two days. Two. A man, who may or may not have had a bad cold and worn a wig, hired a car and drove from Bowness to Heathrow and back in the space of two or three days. Three. This same man is on the passenger list of Thai International as having flown to Hong Kong via Bangkok and back, in two days. Four. This period coincides with the two days that the Prime Minister was asleep virtually incommunicado in the Lake District. Five. During this same period a man known to the Prime Minister was murdered in Hong Kong."

Potts looked at Shaw. "Have I left anything out?"

Shaw took his pipe from his mouth. "Six," he said, "the man called himself Brian Hutchinson and gave a false address."

They sat staring at each other.

"You know what you're saying?" Potts said softly.

Shaw shrugged, "it's only surmise."

"It's bloody preposterous."

"We need something hard."

"Like what?" Potts asked.

"Like proving that Brian Hutchinson doesn't exist and that both his passport and driving licence were false."

"So prove it."

"What about the housekeeper?"

"I'm sure she knows nothing, it would have been the doctor who managed the cover up."

"What about the doctor, have your checked?"

Shaw looked down at the notebook on his knee, "from what I've been able to discover there is nothing in his background that was unusual, other than his friendship with Driver."

"What about his death? I suppose it was natural."

Shaw gave a short mirthless laugh. "I checked that one too. He was very ill, it had only been a matter of when."

Potts got up, roamed around the office and then sat down again.

"What about Driver? Do we know yet when he first met Phillips?"

Shaw shook his head. There was a long silence each busy with his thoughts.

"What do you really think?" Potts said.

Shaw took his time removing his pipe from his mouth then looking steadily at Potts he said, with a gravity that Potts found highly disturbing, "I think the Prime Minister murdered Phillips."

"Oh, Christ," Potts said, bringing his hand sharply down on the desk and breaking the tension, "what do you want to do now?"

"I'd very much like to ask the Prime Minister and see his reactions, but failing that I want to go on digging."

"I want to hear from you at least twice a day. Use anyone or anything you need, but for the moment this is strictly between ourselves. I've got a lot of thinking to do and one or two decisions to make."

Shaw got up and putting his notebook in his pocket said, "you did ask me to find a skeleton in Driver's cupboard."

"I said a skeleton," Potts replied somberly, "not a corpse."

* * *

Sir Hubert Dugdale switched on the television, poured himself a brandy, and sat down as a voice announced 'Viewpoint with Jake Boyle'. The words left the screen to be replaced by a shot of Jake Boyle sitting at a table opposite the Leader of the Opposition.

Dugdale watched and listened as the preliminary introductions were made and then leaned forward as Boyle asked, "tell me Mr. Jowett what is your opinion of the Prime Minister's recent foray into the realms of international diplomacy?"

"I was of course delighted, as I am sure everyone was to see a British Prime Minister once more at the centre of international affairs." Boyle waited a moment until he realised that Jowett had finished.

"Do you feel Mr. Jowett, that if you had been Prime Minister at this time, you would have had a similar success?"

Jowett smiled slowly, "that, Mr. Boyle, if I may say so would be pure speculation."

"Speculation that you would have done as well or

144

speculation that you could be Prime Minister," Boyle interjected quickly.

The smile vanished from Jowett's face, "I suggest that we move on to the important issues facing this country, that I am here to discuss," he said stiffly.

Dugdale sighed as he saw Jowett repeatedly made to look inept by Boyle. He switched off the set and lay back in his chair, unconsciously fingering the deep scratch on his face.

He had become increasingly aware that he had sadly misjudged Jowett. He suspected that the man had no real burning desire to become Prime Minister and he felt certain that he would not go beyond what he termed 'his bounds of decency', to achieve his ambitions. His conclusion comforted him as he thought of Fiona Reid waiting for the exposure of the Prime Minister that would never come. That would hurt her far more than anything else he could do, and after Driver's recent exploits and Jowett's television performance tonight, he realised that in any case he would have great difficulty in seriously damaging Driver to the benefit of Jowett.

His musings were broken by the ringing of the telephone. He levered himself out of the easy chair and walked over to the desk.

"Yes?" As he listened to his editor his eyes began to glitter. "You'd better come over at once."

He stood with his hand on the telephone and suddenly gave a high pitched laugh. What was it his mother used to say, 'when one door closes, another one opens'.

* * *

"What does he want?" the Prime Minister asked wearily.

"He wouldn't say, but he was most insistent,"

145

Andrew Blaine replied, "he said he would come at any time that was suitable to you, the sooner the better."

"Is Don Parrish about?"

"I think so."

"Ask him to come up, I'll see if he has any idea."

"That's it then," Blaine said gathering his folders together. You're pretty much up to date with the paperwork."

"Thank God for that. I knew it was piling up while I was away, but not to such a degree."

The Prime Minister stretched as his secretary left the sitting room, and thought that he had never been so tired since — since Hong Kong. He swiftly brushed the thought away.

What a week it had been and everything had happened so fast. But this is what it was like at the top — at the real top. The issues were so great, the implications so vast, that if anything was distorted, the world knew about it. And he had certainly been in the thick of it he thought with pride. But why him? Destiny? He laughed outright at his foolishness, but the thought persisted. What if he had not spoken to Provitch? What if he had not been friendly with Sloane? What if? Would there have been a war? Annihilation?

The knock on the door brought him back to reality.

"Ah Don — Good Lord, you look worse than I do."

"Is that meant to make me feel better?" Parrish said with a tired grin. "It's still pretty chaotic with the aftermath of the trip. Every reporter in the world seems to have one question he wants answering about you, and some of them are pretty bizarre I can tell you."

The Prime Minister laughed and then said seriously "you did a good job, Don, and I'm grateful. I shan't forget it."

The Press Secretary looked embarrassed and then said, "you wanted to see me?"

"It's about Sir Hubert Dugdale. He wants a meeting urgently. Do you have any idea why?"

"No. Can't think of anything. Unless he's ready to change sides."

"What sort of chap is he? I've only met him formally."

Don Parrish hesitated and looked away. He was uneasy about repeating gossip concerning a newspaper proprietor who was about to see the Prime Minister. Especially the type of gossip he had heard.

"Don are you holding out on me?" the Prime Minister demanded, looking shrewdly at the elegant figure of his Press Secretary.

"Not holding out exactly, but there's been a bit of gossip and I'm not sure just how true it is."

"Give."

"It concerns Sir Hubert's sexual . . ." he paused searching for a word, "proclivities."

The Prime Minister was looking at him with huge enjoyment. "I can hardly wait."

"He likes beating up women."

"Now that's not funny. Not funny at all," he said becoming serious.

"In fact," Parrish went on, "the rumour is, that a young lady is at this moment in intensive care with only a fifty-fifty chance of pulling through."

"Where has the rumour come from?"

"The young lady's flat-mate."

"I see. So it's more than a rumour?"

"I believe that a large amount of money is in the process of changing hands to ensure the future of the young lady and her flat-mate, on the understanding that the matter is not taken any further."

"Nasty. Are the police involved?"

"Not that I know of. It's on the press grapevine because a reporter on a Sunday newspaper was approached by the flat-mate who thought she could make some money by selling the story. She showed him diaries and one or two other things implicating Sir Hubert, but on their second meeting she retracted the lot, hinting she would lose a fortune if he pursued it."

"And I suppose the fact that Sir Hubert owns a newspaper encouraged the reporter to drop it."

"I'm not sure that's quite fair," Parrish said, "but I'm too tired to argue the point."

"Is Dugdale still close to Jowett?"

"As far as I know."

"How much does he interfere with his editor — what's his name?"

"Potts. Doesn't appear to interfere, but it's always a subtle relationship, difficult to separate a suggestion from an instruction."

"Oh well, I'd better see him. Ask him to come early tomorrow morning, you can even suggest breakfast. That won't upset any of the others will it?"

Parrish smiled, pleased that the Prime Minister had taken notice of his repeated requests for him not to appear to be more partial to one newspaper than to another.

"I don't think so. They all know that Sir Hubert is no particular friend of yours."

CHAPTER 17

Sir Hubert Dugdale shook hands with the Prime Minister. "It's very good of you to see me at such short notice and it was kind of you to invite me for this," he waved his hand over the table laid for breakfast in the dining room of the Prime Minister's flat at Downing Street into which he had just been ushered.

"I'm afraid it was the only time I could manage, and I gathered there was some urgency." The Prime Minister sat down and reached for the toast.

"Well, I considered it urgent, but of course it depends on how you feel about it."

"Well go ahead. We won't be disturbed, that's why we're helping ourselves." He poured a cup of coffee for the tall man who had a large scratch down the side of his face.

Dugdale took a sip of coffee, observed the Prime Minister carefully, and said, "Mrs. Fiona Reid has been to see me a couple of times." He watched as the Prime Minister put down his cup of coffee dabbed his mouth with his napkin and said, "I see." The tone was non-committal but Dugdale fancied that the Prime Minister had tensed. He went on, "she appears to feel aggrieved about, what she terms, the shabby treatment she and her husband have received since his unfortunate suicide attempt."

The Prime Minister was toying with a spoon, but remained silent.

"In fact," Dugdale said, "she has some preposterous story that you were involved in her husband's downfall, and quite frankly," he said lowering his voice, "she is out to destroy you. I thought you should know as soon as possible."

"How unfortunate," the Prime Minister said, once more taking up his coffee cup.

"Unfortunate?"

"Yes. I knew that Fiona had taken Peter's resignation badly, but I didn't think she was this upset. What has she been saying."

Dugdale gave a short laugh. "It's hardly worth repeating, it's so unbelievable, and I've made it quite clear that neither I nor anyone else would publish such rubbish."

The Prime Minister looked at him warily, "I would have thought," he said matter of factly, "that you would rather have enjoyed causing me, shall we say, embarrassment?"

"Really, Mr. Prime Minister, I honestly feel you do me an injustice. Fair political comment is one thing, a criminal smear is another. Anyway," he went on, "I don't think that you can criticise the Globe recently for being antagonistic towards you."

"No. I must say that your coverage of my trips to Russia and America were most fair."

"I wasn't thinking only of your recent travels," Dugdale said leaning back in his chair and looking around the room. "If I may say so, with the greatest respect, I think you are doing a fine job. In fact I think it would be bad for the country if there was any change of government at the next election."

The Prime Minister looked at him with frank surprise, then said, "that's most kind of you, Sir Hubert. I would value your support.

"However," Dugdale said, not looking at the Prime Minister, "there would be one or two points on which I should like to be satisfied . . ."

"Points?"

"Yes, one or two minor shifts of policy, which I should like to suggest."

"I am always pleased to receive suggestions," the

Prime Minister said, "but of course I can't guarantee to act on them."

The Prime Minister did not interrupt as Dugdale spoke for several minutes outlining his proposals. There was a long silence when he had finished.

"You must realise, that most of what you have just said it totally unacceptable to me," the Prime Minister said coldly, "and quite frankly I can't think why you should think I would even be interested."

Dugdale appeared unperturbed. "As we shall now be working closer together, I thought . . ."

"What gave you that idea?" the Prime Minister interjected.

Dugdale looked directly at the Prime Minister and said, "I believe in being realistic, as I'm sure you do, you need my support and there are certain assurances I require before I am prepared to give it."

"I don't wish to be arrogant, Sir Hubert, but I don't think I need your support. I would welcome it — yes, but that's a totally different matter."

"Oh I think you misunderstand me Prime Minister, I wasn't referring solely to my newspaper's support for you politically, I was thinking more of my handling Mrs. Reid for you and matters relating to that unfortunate episode."

"What are you implying?" I'm not sure that I like your tone or whatever it is that you are trying to say."

"It is very simple. Mrs. Reid made several allegations against you and in the investigation of them certain interesting facts emerged."

"Are you trying to blackmail me, Sir Hubert?" the Prime Minister said quietly as he pushed his chair from the table and stood up.

Dugdale remained seated. "Of course not. All I am suggesting is that in return for silencing Fiona Reid, by putting about that her allegations have been well investigated and proved groundless, as far as the press are concerned, you would . . .

The Prime Minister stood looking down at Dugdale. "I've nothing to hide and there's nothing that Fiona Reid can say that can be taken seriously so I am afraid I'm at rather a loss to understand you." He looked pointedly at his watch, "now, I really must get ready for my next appointment."

Dugdale did not move. He was impressed with the Prime Minister's apparent calm and thought it time to try and jolt him out of it.

"I wonder," he said blandly, "if the name Brian Hutchinson means anything to you?" The result of his question was beyond his wildest expectation.

The Prime Minister went white and momentarily swayed. He clutched the back of the chair in which he had previously been sitting and then almost collapsed into it.

Dugdale poured a fresh cup of coffee into the Prime Minister's cup and offered it to him, but the Prime Minister ignored him and continued to stare into space.

"I see that the name registers," Dugdale said, putting down the cup of coffee. The Prime Minister was breathing heavily and Dugdale watched him fight for control. Eventually the Prime Minister said, "that's a name from the past."

For a moment Dugdale looked puzzled then he realised that the Prime Minister was already attempting to bluff his way out of his obvious predicament.

"No, Prime Minister not the past, not unless you consider last August the past."

"I don't know what you're talking about, and I don't think you do either."

"Try me," and when the Prime Minister remained silent he went on, "Windermere, Hong Kong, Phillips, Windermere."

The Prime Minister was staring at him with an unbelieving look on his face.

"Dr. Firth must have been a very good friend indeed to stick out his neck like he did."

"Has — has — all — this — this nonsense come from Fiona Reid?" the Prime Minister stammered.

"No, not all of it. She just put us on the right track."

"Us?" the Prime Minister said quickly, beginning to regain his composure.

"One or two of us at the Globe," Dugdale said airily waving his hand.

"Who is this Phillips you mentioned?"

"Enough," Dugdale said in a hard voice, "I thought you were implicated in the death of Albert Phillips in Hong Kong a few weeks ago and from the way in which you behaved this morning, I am now convinced of it."

The Prime Minister made a poor attempt at a laugh. "I really think you have taken leave of your senses, if this outrageous story were true, why haven't you gone to the police?"

"We have not reached that stage yet."

"So you are trying to blackmail me. Apart from your ridiculous political 'suggestions' what else are you hoping for. Influence? Money? I think I begin to understand. You no longer think that Jowett, whom you had in your pocket, now has a chance of winning the next election, so you have fabricated this non-sensical story in order to try and have influence with me." He snorted contemptuously, and Dugdale admired his nerve.

"You haven't denied it." Dugdale said quietly.

"Denied what? You've got some half-baked idea and you expect me to treat it seriously?"

"Well then," Dugdale said getting up, "if you think it's only half-baked I'd better go away and let it cook a little longer."

He moved towards the door, a smile on his face.

"Where did you get that scratch?" the Prime

Minister said suddenly.

Dugdale looked at him sharply, "what scratch?" he said, as his hand involuntarily reached for his face.

The Prime Minister nodded to himself as if agreeing with the decision he had just made.

"Did you get it from one of your women?"

Dugdale paled and his eyes began to glitter.

"Did one of them fight back? Was it perhaps the one who's in intensive care? Is that why she's there, because she did that?"

Dugdale was trembling with fury. "Don't you dare try to smear me just because you're in a jam," he said his voice rising, "I won't have it."

"Won't you?" the Prime Minister said, once more in full command of himself. "I think I have far more hard facts to go on than you do."

"I'm talking about murder," Dugdale spat out.

"I'd pray if I were you, that the young lady makes it otherwise, I too will be talking about murder," the Prime Minister said calmly.

Dugdale stood glaring and then not concealing his anger, he said, "I came here to offer help and advice. You have questioned my motives and made damaging personal allegations. I am prepared to forgive you, knowing how much I must have shocked you with what I had to say. But I am warning you, in our future meetings you will have to be more sensible, if you wish to be certain of my support — and my silence."

He jerked open the door and leaving it open behind him, strode from the room.

The Prime Minister felt totally drained of energy. He walked over to the door and closed it, then went back to the table and put his head in his hands.

He had been completely shattered when Dugdale had mentioned the name of Brian Hutchinson. It was as if a searchlight had been suddenly directed into the darkest part of his mind, temporarily blinding and numbing him:

That the light had been shone by Dugdale had only increased his shock. He had quickly seen where the talk about Fiona Reid was leading but he had never imagined for one moment that Dugdale would have the whole story.

He tried to focus his mind on what he should do next, but he found himself transfixed by the knowledge which Dugdale possessed. How had he obtained it?

The Reids knew nothing. Firth and Phillips were dead. He had covered all his tracks. So how had it been put together.

The case! It had to be the case that he had left in the Boat House. But that would not have revealed the name he had used. He had destroyed the passport and driving licence the night he had returned to Downing Street, so no one could have found them. Anyway they had been obtained for him by Phillips — and Phillips was dead.

It was all going to come out, just now, when he was at a peak of international acclaim, and all because Peter Reid had become involved with Phillips and because Fiona Reid was a bitch.

But how had Dugdale found out, and what would he do now? It was obvious the man wanted power, the hidden power of the number one advisor. He had temporily blocked him, by his knowledge of the young woman in hopsital, but if Dugdale could successfully buy her silence, that affair would be closed.

No. He was finished. If Dugdale knew so much, Meeling could not be far behind. He had thought that he had stopped the Security Chief from probing any further, but now he doubted it — and what had the bloody man been doing at Blackpool?

He inwardly groaned at the thought that Dugdale had replaced Phillips as the only man in the world with a hold over him. But was he the only one. Hadn't he

said something about 'one or two people at the Globe'?
Could he silence them or was he bluffing and ensuring
some protection for himself at the same time? And how
did he hope to silence the other newspapers as he had
promised? Only if he was certain that Fiona did not
know the whole story and that he was able to prevent
the rest of the information from reaching anyone else.

He was startled when Andrew Blaine's voice said,
"are you all right?"

He jerked his head out of his hands and snapped,
"don't you knock any more?"

"I did Sir, twice," Blaine said stiffly, "I knew you
were in here and I was becoming alarmed."

"You're an old woman," the Prime Minister said,
but his intended jocularity was missing from his voice
and he saw that his secretary was deeply offended.

"I'm sorry Andy, it's just that I don't feel too well."

"Shall I ring Doctor Conway?" Blaine said immediately concerned.

"What's the 'List' for this morning?"

Blaine quickly consulted a copy of the List that was
on top of the folders he was carrying.

"I could juggle things around until three, it would
get trickier after that."

"I think you'd better do so," the Prime Minister said
wearily, "I'm going back to bed. I don't think it's anything more than being overtired. You'd better send for
Conway just the same."

"Right away. Leave everything to me and don't
worry," Blaine fussed.

The Prime Minister walked out of the dining room
down the corridor and into his bedroom. He got un-
dressed put on his pyjamas and climbed into bed. He
had not done this since he was a child, he thought, as he
pulled the bedclothes under his chin. In those days
when things got too much for him, he had taken to his
bed hoping that 'the Nasty' would have gone away by

156

the time he had to get up. He gave a deep sigh as he realised that this time no matter how long he stayed in
bed, this particular 'Nasty' would still be there.

CHAPTER 18

Roger Shaw stared at his editor in astonishment, but Potts refused to meet his eye.

"What exactly do you mean, 'leave it for the moment?' he asked, a trace of anger in his voice.

"It means what it says," Potts said with half-hearted belligerence.

"But, for God's sake why? We're practically there. It'll be a sensation," Shaw said with genuine bewilderment.

"Look, Roger," Potts said, and Shaw's eyebrows fractionally rose at the unaccustomed use of his first name. "There are one or two other factors involved which I can't tell you about just yet."

"Like what?"

"I've just said, I can't tell you."

"Are we being muzzled?" Shaw asked very deliberately.

Potts glowered at Shaw, "no one muzzles me," he growled, but Shaw found him unconvincing.

"You'll have to tell me more if you want to persuade me," he said.

"I don't have to persuade you," Potts said in his usual brusque tones, "I tell you."

"Not this time," Shaw said firmly.

"What the hell do you mean?"

"Unless I get a satisfactory explanation for your extraordinary decision to kill the hottest story I've ever had or ever likely to have, you can have my resignation now and I'll take the story somewhere else."

Shaw waited for the explosion and was amazed when Potts said quietly, "I don't blame you. Not one little bit. I'd feel exactly the same in your shoes."

"So what's it all about?"

"Security."

"Whose security?"

Potts sighed, "I told him I'd probably have to tell you and he agreed but only as a last resort. I consider this the last resort."

"Who's he?"

"The Prime Minister," Potts said quietly.

Shaw looked dumbfounded.

"You've spoken to him about this?" he managed to blurt out. "You've actually asked him?"

Potts nodded unhappily.

"Christ Almighty, what did you expect him to say?" Shaw went on angrily, "oh dear you've discovered my little secret — yes I murdered Mr. Phillips in Hong Kong."

"That's enough," Potts snapped. "It wasn't like that at all. Sir Hubert spoke to him," he raised his hand as Shaw was about to speak, "he is the proprietor, he first put us on to the Reid affair, and I kept him constantly informed of our progress."

"So the lead came from him," Shaw said, in a calmer voice.

"Yes, and when I told him your theory, he thought it best to see what he could find out at the source."

"He thought," Shaw said flatly.

"Well, I must confess I wasn't altogether happy about it, but it did make some sort of sense, and as it's turned out it's a good job we did otherwise we could have been in all sorts of trouble with the security angle."

"Terrific," Shaw said.

"Do you want to know the story, or would you prefer to carry on with your sarcasm?"

Shaw shrugged, "it hardly seems to matter now that the decision has been made to kill it."

"I know how you feel, but you see Brian Hutchinson

wasn't the Prime Minister."

"So who was he — Donald Duck?"

"He was an agent of the Security Services who reported to the Prime Minister not only before he left on a highly sensitive operation to Hong Kong but also on his return."

Shaw gave a loud guffaw. "The Prime Minister told you that — and you believe it?"

"He has given all the details to Sir Hubert who is totally satisfied. When Sir Hubert saw how unhappy I was about the whole affair he arranged a meeting with the Prime Minister who confirmed it himself. I gave him my undertaking that we would forget that you had stumbled across the name of Brian Hutchinson."

Shaw was still smiling in disbelief.

"I told them that you would be hard to convince," Potts went on, "and they agreed that if necessary I could put you in the picture."

"Do you know the nature of the job Hutchinson was on?"

"No."

"Would it be possible to meet Hutchinson?"

"No."

"Do you believe this . . . this . . .garbage?"

Potts did not answer. He felt tired and he felt old. He was also depressed when he saw the fire and energy in Shaw, and realised that he himself had become so cynical that he could not raise the passion over this business that he would have done years ago. He was by no means convinced. But what could he do in the face of his proprietor and the Prime Minister? Call them both liars and stalk out of Number 10 Downing Street? The very location of the meeting had given a great deal of psychological authority to their statement.

He had pressed as far as he could, but short of calling the Prime Minister a murderer to his face, and pressing a line of enquiry there was nothing he could do except

160

resign. And then what? If he couldn't get anywhere as editor of a powerful daily newspaper, what progress would he make as an out of work journalist. Also, he had reasoned, it could very well be true. It certainly made more sense than that the Prime Minister had donned a wig, slipped out of the country and murdered someone in Hong Kong.

It would be different if the doctor had still been alive, there sould have been something to go on. But now? What had worried him the most, had been the not too subtle hint of a reward for his 'services to journalism' being in the pipeline. It could well have been true, but it concerned him more than anything else. Not so much that it was a possible bribe but that he may have already been seduced by the idea.

When all was said and done, at its best a story was a nine days' wonder, and over the years he had had many of them, but a knighthood lasted a lifetime. He angrily brushed the thought away.

"Do you believe it?" Shaw repeated.

"It could be true and certainly for the moment I think we should cool it. Of one thing I'm certain, no one else is going to break it, and if anyone looks like doing so, we've got more than a head start. But for now save it."

"For what?"

"You never know," Potts said reaching for the top file in his in tray.

"No you don't, do you?" Shaw said as he got up and left the room.

* * *

Sir Hubert Dugdale breathed a sigh of relief as he replaced the telephone. He had needed increasing courage to make his daily call to the hospital posing as a reporter from the Globe, to enquire as to the progress

161

of Maxine Lambert. At last he had received the news he had been waiting for, 'out of danger and making satisfactory progress'.

He braced his shoulders and felt that the overall situation was looking up.

He had not been altogether surprised at the Prime Minister's call late yesterday, and had at once gone to Downing Street as requested.

The Prime Minister had appeared to be his normal self and had explained his reaction at breakfast that morning as being one of shock at hearing an extremely sensitive security name, Brian Hutchinson, being spoken by a newspaper proprietor.

He had listened sceptically as the Prime Minister had gone on to explain 'as much as he could under the circumstances'.

When he had finished the Prime Minister had apologised for his reference to the 'injured girl', and admitted that he would value a continuing association between them.

Dugdale smiled and preened a little as he recalled the Prime Minister's strong indication that the House of Lords might well benefit from his presence. He knew that he had furthered his aims with Driver more in one day than he had with Jowett during several years of supporting the opposition leader.

He had been gracious in his acknowledgement of the Prime Minister's apologies, grave in his acceptance of the explanations regarding Hutchinson and co-operative in framing a suitable version for Potts and Shaw. It was also at his prompting that a suitable inducement to Potts, to encourage him to drop the case had been devised. All in all it had been most satisfactory, thought Dugdale as he sat down at his desk. What had appeared, only yesterday, to be a catastrophic end to his ambitions, had proved by the end of the day to have been a triumphant beginning to them.

* * *

"Listen, Hubert, you don't have to say any more. I understand. As for the information you're worried about, I've forgotten it. Good-bye."

Paul Jowett knew that he should be hurt, angry and dismayed by the telephone call but all he felt was relief. Relief that his association with Dugdale was apparently at an end. He had sensed a change in the newspaper proprietor's attitude over the last few days, the hitherto daily telephone calls having almost ceased and the stream of memoranda offering advice on every subject having all but dried up. He had assumed that Dugdale was just preoccupied with the Phillips business which had become an obsession with him, but the telephone call had revealed that Dugdale had obviously been in the process of going over to Driver.

He realised that his relief was due to the knowledge that he would no longer have to wade in the sludge that Dugdale had seemed determined to stir. It was not his style and he had become increasingly ashamed at the depths to which he had allowed Dugdale to drag him.

He could not bring himself to believe that Driver, whom he admired, would be so foolish as to be as involved as Dugdale imagined, nor did he feel himself capable of using the information even if it was true.

The Prime Minister was now a highly respected international figure. A man who had lifted Britain's prestige throughout the world and who seemed poised to rise much further to the benefit of his country as well as to himself.

So what purpose would be served by a colossal smear. It would more than likely rebound on the perpetrator of the smear and leave Driver virtually untouched.

He walked into the bedroom. His wife already in bed looked up from her book. "Who was that on the phone at this time? There's nothing wrong is there?"

He sat on the edge of her bed and told her everything enjoying the way her eyes widened like a child's at certain parts of his story. When he had finished, she took his hands in hers and looked him straight in the eyes, "you're a good man Paul. A very good man."

"A good man or a foolish one, Molly?"

"Well, that depends on what you do next."

"What do you think I should do?"

"Do you really have to ask?"

"No. I suppose not. But I should have liked to have been Prime Minister," he said wistfully.

"Leave it to the youngsters, Paul, it's important to them."

"And not to you — to us?"

"No dear. I think we're both old enough to know that there are much more important things in life than power."

"Like the grandchildren?" he asked with a smile.

"Like us," she said looking at him fondly.

CHAPTER 19

The Prime Minister pretending to be immersed in his papers, waited for Sir John Meeling to leave the room. When the door had closed behind him the Prime Minister threw down his pen and gave a large sigh of relief. He felt that he had handled the interview exceptionally well. But this time he had been prepared.

He had been surprised when the Security Chief had requested the meeting and from his evasiveness, the Prime Minister had gathered that it once more concerned Phillips.

He had carefully gone over in his mind every possible reason for Meeling wanting the meeting. He strongly suspected from his two conversations with Dugdale, that the Globe people had not found the case. If, therefore, Meeling, in spite of strict instructions from the Home Secretary, was still wanting to see him, it could be that he had somehow or other discovered the case. He had considered several possible reactions but in the end had opted for a blank denial of ever having seen or heard of the case — and it had worked.

He sat back in his chair at the table and let his eyes rove around the beautiful Cabinet Room. To think that Albert Phillips had nearly ruined it all. The bloody man had almost been as much trouble dead as he had been alive. All those years of waiting for him to talk as he became increasingly fond of alcohol. Waiting for him to tell someone who believed, or wanted to believe him, how the British Prime Minister had got hold of his first money. The money that was the basis of his future fortune. The money that had enabled him to become Prime Minister.

He shifted uncomfortably in his chair as he tried to brush away the invading images from so long ago when he had been barely twenty years old. But today they would not go. It was like a silent picture. The old Chinaman arguing with Phillips over the price of the tiny bags of white powder on the table. Phillips pulling the gun. The flash. The noise. The blood and gore as the Chinaman's head was blown apart. He almost felt now the horror he had felt then. There had been no fear no guilt, just horror at what Phillips had done, followed by the surprise of finding that Phillips had a gun.

In his mind he saw Phillips scooping up the bags of powder and stuffing them into his pockets, as he shouted for him to do the same.

The had got away. Just the two of them. No one else had ever known. They had left Hong Kong and smuggled the drugs to Bangkok. There Phillips had gone out one morning and come back an hour later with fistfulls of money. The next day they had separated.

It was when he had just been elected to parliament that Phillips had re-entered his life and demanded money.

Then when he had become Prime Minister Phillips had sent him a congratulatory message to 'their continued good fortune' and demanded more money. It was then that he decided that he had to kill Phillips. He would have to do it himself, so that it would all be finally over and no one else in the world would have a hold over him. It had also become apparent to him that Phillips was drinking heavily and that it was only going to be a matter of time before he said something.

He phoned him and told him that he was sending a trusted emissary called Walker, who, whilst not knowing the reasons for the payment, was authorised to negotiate one very large final sum of money.

He got up from his chair and stretched. He must now

concentrate on the future, on the political problems that were now his concern. It had all been a colossal gamble and he must not waste the freedom of action and the peace of mind, that he had won. The ringing of the telephone startled him, and brought him swiftly back to reality. He frowned when the operator told him that Sir Hubert Dugdale wished to speak to him. The man had become a damned nuisance, he thought, as he sat back prepared for a long harangue from the newspaper proprietor.

It annoyed him that Dugdale had a hold over him, even though it was slender and difficult to prove. But it was sufficient for him to have to listen whenever Dugdale decided to speak.

As the voice droned on, an idea slowly began to form and he started to smile.

It just might work, the Prime Minister thought, and with Dugdale dead he really would be free.

Books in the Dedalus Modern Fiction and European Classics Series are available at your local bookshop or newsagent, or can be ordered direct from the publisher by writing to Dedalus Cash Sales, 9 St. Stephen's Terrace, London SW8 1DJ.
Please enclose remittance to the value of the cover price.

Titles currently available include:

The Travelling Men — Eric Lane	£2.50
The Arabian Nightmare — Robert Irwin	£2.95
The Revenants — Geoffrey Farrington	£2.50
Mastro Don Gesualdo — Giovanni Verga	£2.95
Short Sicilian Novels — Giovanni Verga	£2.50
Oberammergau: A Passion Play	
	£3.95

THE TRAVELLING MEN — Eric Lane

The pictures in the brochure are of Roy, he's the one with the microphone, and Giacomo the goodlooking one driving the coach. Join them and enjoy the merry go-round world of Rover Tours. They are the professionals, whose job it is to cope with the formalities: the four hour wait at the frontier, the violence of the border police, the strikes, burglaries and motorway accidents which occur while you sit back and enjoy your holiday.

"Never a dull moment on this tour," said Mr. Vashi, as Roy and Giocomo drink three bottles of wine during their coffee break. They will help you with your problems, if you are young and pretty, like Anne, or even middle-aged and available like Mrs. Cain. Let them worry about the dangerous psychopath who is pursuing the tour round Europe. This after all is what they are paid for.

After this holiday a coach tour will never seem the same again.

THE REVENANTS — (a Gothic Fantasy) — Geoffrey Farrington

A family curse reaches through time to damn a young man in Victorian Cornwall. The Revenant is possessed with supernatural life and power, but tainted by morbid desires and marked by human despair. The horror of being itself and the fear of the normal are sensitively conveyed in an atmosphere of growing and claustrophobic terror. The classic themes of Terror Literature rise once more to haunt you in The Revenants.

THE ARABIAN NIGHMARE — Robert Irwin

The Arabian Nightmare conjures up the fantastic world of the Arabian Nights. The Nightmare pervades Medieval Cairo. It haunts its labyrinthine streets. It is a dream without awakening, a flight without escape, a tale without end. Balian of Norwich is pursued through a maze of speaking apes, sultans, seductresses and ghouls. The Arabian Nightmare is a guide to the Orient of the mind.

Also available from Robert Irwin:

The Dreadlord (a novel about the Wars of the Roses)

Dedalus European Classics

MASTRO-DON GESUALDO — Giovanni Verga (translated by
D. H. Lawrence)

On the face of things, Mastro-Don Gesualdo is a success. Born a peasant
but a man 'with an eye for everything going', he becomes one of the richest
men in Sicily, marrying an aristocrat with his daughter destined, in time, to
wed a duke.

But Gesualdo falls foul of the rigid class structure in mid-19th century
Sicily. His title 'Mastro-Don', 'Worker-Gentlemen', is ironic in itself.
Peasants and gentry alike resent his extraordinary success. And when the
pattern of society is threatened by revolt, Gesualdo is the rebels' first target.

Published in 1888, Verga's classic was first introduced to this country in
1925 by D. H. Lawrence in its own superb translation. Although broad in
scope, with a large cast and covering over twenty years, *Mastro-Don
Gesualdo* is exact and concentrated: it cuts from set-piece to set-piece —
from feast-day to funeral to sun white stubble fields — anticipating the
narrative techniques of the cinema.

SHORT SICILIAN NOVELS — Giovanni Verga (translated by
D. H. Lawrence)

"The Little Novels of Sicily have that sense of the wholeness of life, the
spare exuberance, the endless inflections and overtones, and the
magnificent and thrilling vitality of major literature."
– New York Times

"In these stories the whole Sicily of the eighteen-sixties lives before us —
poor gentry, priests, rich landowners, farmers, peasants, animals, seasons
and scenery; and whether his subject be the brutal bloodshed of an abortive
revolution or the simple human comedy that can even attend deep
mourning. Verga never loses his complete artistic mastery of his material.
He throws the whole of his pity into the intensity of his art, and with the
simplicity only attainable by genius lays bare beneath all the seat and tears
and clamour of day-to-day humanity those mysterious 'mortal things
which touch the minds'.
– Times Literary Supplement.

Also by Giovanni Verga a new translation of I Malavoglia available from
Dedalus in 1985.